INTRODUCTION

Ed Page

On my frequent trips to the liquor store, the adorable neighborhood children always crowd around me in the street, tugging at my pants and shoelaces, and beg to once again hear the tale of me, Aaron, Shya, and Steven, a tale I call "Three Men and a Baby" (just kidding, Steven). I remind the children that they've heard it many times, and that, while thrilling, it is a tale both long and entirely factual, and that I really should be getting to the liquor store, as I'm having lunch with a Captain Morgan and I don't want to keep him waiting. This always evokes a lot of booing, but I shush the children and tell them I prefer "boos" I can drink. With that, I shake free of their little fingers and continue briskly down the avenue. Before I know it, I'm drunk. Three days later, I wake up in a parking lot, lying in a puddle of what appears to be apple Snapple but which doesn't taste like apple Snapple at all. As I stagger homeward, I encounter the neighborhood children again, and, since I'm weak and my defenses are lowered, they always succeed in selling me expensive swampland on Neptune. I must own half the planet by now. They also succeed in getting me to tell them the tale of me, Aaron, Shya, and Steven, a tale I call "The Four Wise Men" (just kidding, Steven). In fact, this happened just this morning. I sat on the stoop in front of an apartment building in Seattle's beautiful Capitol Hill district, the children – their little faces rosy with anticipation – sat on the stairs and sidewalk around me, and I began my tale, a tale I call "Hair" (just kidding, Aaron).

"My dear, sweet children," I began. "As most of you already know, Aaron, Shya, Steven, and I have known each other much longer than is humanly normal. Our story begins on a sunny day in the spring of 1842. I was down by the ol' fishin' hole with Bessie Lou, which is what I called my lucky fishin' pole. I'd whittled her myself out of a giant oak that had been struck by lightning the previous winter. The tree had fallen on my grandpapa and killed him very painfully. Grandpapa was a wicked old cuss who got what he deserved. He used to whup my snow-white bottom just to watch it turn red. Honestly, the man was worse than castor oil.

"Bessie Lou and I, on the other hand, got along

famously. She kept my belly full of catfish and I, in turn, kept her long, elegant neck free of termites and beavers. Or, at least, I tried to. As I sat there on that fine spring day waiting for her to catch me a big, tasty catfish, a giant beaver with fire in its eyes leapt out of the fishin' hole and tore Bessie Lou from my grasp. The bucktoothed demon plopped into the water and began swimming away, my beloved Bessie Lou trapped in its evil mouth. 'Oh, Bessie Lou!' I hollered. 'Come back! That beaver doesn't love you like I do!' Of course, I could have gone after that infernal creature and saved my darling pole had I ever learned how to swim. Alas, I never had."

"You didn't know how to swim, Uncle Ed?" It was one of the neighborhood children, a little girl named Marjory.

"No, Marjory, I didn't. I was too frightened by stories of sea monsters and water tigers to ever dip so much as a toe into any body of water. I wouldn't even take baths."

"Wow, Uncle Ed," said little Marjory, "you sure were a wussy!"

"No more interruptions, children. So, anyways, there I was watching helplessly as a beaver swam away with my beautiful fishin' pole. Suddenly, out of nowhere, a boy I'd never seen before dived into the fishin' hole and swam like a flash after that beaver. He caught it and stabbed it in the eye with a huge knife and brought Bessie Lou back to me safe and sound.

"'Wow, thanks, violent stranger!' I exclaimed.

"'Think nothing of it,' he said. Then, holding up the beaver carcass, he added, 'Now let's go find the local hatsmith and make a couple of top hats out of this rod-filching fiend.'

"A few hours later, we emerged from the hatter's shop crowned like millionaires.

"'Well, what should we do now?' asked the violent stranger.

"'How 'bout we steal some whiskey from my old man's liquor cabinet?' I suggested. 'He's got some stuff in there called Captain Morgan's. It tastes just like a dream, no foolin'.'

"'Now, that does sound mighty fine,' the violent stranger replied, 'but I think I have an even better idea: what say we go hop on the back of Peggy, my magical winged horse, and fly to the ends of time?'

"'Can I bring the Captain Morgan's with us?' I said.

"'I reckon,' he replied.

"'Okay!' I said. 'I'll be right back!'

"When I got back with the whiskey, the violent stranger led me to his flying horse, which he'd tied to a tree not far from the fishin' hole. She was pure black and her wings were huge and beautiful. I put Bessie Lou and the booze in a saddlebag, and climbed into the saddle, which had places for two riders. The stranger sat in front, I in back. At the stranger's command, Peggy spread her wings and away we went, high into the air and deep into the past.

"We flew back to the beginning of time and watched the big bang happen. Then we went back before the big bang, which was a real mindblower. Unfortunately, it's impossible to describe. We visited the time of the dinosaurs, too. The interesting thing about the dinosaurs is that they were all that bright orange color that hunters wear.

"Then we traveled to the time of the New Testament. I shared the Captain Morgan's with Jesus and he said it was the best thing he ever tasted. He transformed the Sea of Galilee into Captain Morgan's whiskey and said, 'Whosoever believeth in me, go nuts.'

"Then I asked the violent stranger about the future.

"'Does the human species ever die out?' I wondered.

"'Why, yes,' he said. 'That happens in the twenty-first century as a direct result of a man named George W. Bush, who almost single-handedly destroys the earth and all its inhabitants.'

"'Wow,' I said. 'That fella must be a real pain in the britches. Let's go check him out.'

"When we arrived in the twenty-first century – atop Mt. Rainier, for some reason – Peggy announced that she was tired of flying around through time and that she was really a man trapped inside the body of a magical flying horse. There was a puff of smoke and suddenly Peggy was gone and Shya was standing there.

"'Hi, I'm Shya,' he said.

"This reminded the violent stranger that he'd forgotten to tell me his name.

"'Sorry, I'm such an ass,' he said. 'My name's Aaron.'

"So that's the story, children."

"Wait," said Chester, little Marjory's even littler brother. "You forgot about Steven. How did you meet Steven?"

"Oh, right – Steven," I said. "To tell you the truth, I don't have any idea how I met Steven. I must have run into him at the liquor store."

"Wait – what's the moral of the story?" It was Marjory.

"The moral of the story is that you ask too many questions. I'm sleepy. I'm going to go home and get some shut-eye."

And that's exactly what I did.

TABLE OF CONTENTS

ELIZABETH & THE EVIL DZOKIO

Elizabeth Alexander

Once upon a time, not so very long ago, a cranky little maiden awoke with a mountain in her mind. Elizabeth had seen that mountain somewhere before. She could tell by the summit. The mountain's hairdo, a windswept plume, was unmistakable.

On the west face was a glacial valley basin. In the center of the basin was a nametag, rooted in a crevasse. "Churning goddess of the ocean, Lady goddess of the wind, Mother goddess of the universe," the nametag read.

"This doesn't ring a bell," muttered Elizabeth. "Unless...I didn't sleep with you in college, did I?" she demanded.

The mountain rolled her eyes. "My name is Everest," she said. "Sagarmatha in Nepali."

"Omigod."

"Look at me, Elizabeth," the mountain said.

It is no small thing deliberately and explicitly to invite a person's gaze.

Elizabeth looked close & closer still and as she looked, her eyes softened. Her shoulders dropped. Her breathing slowed.

"Come and visit," said the mountain. "Come to Nepal."

Elizabeth was on the verge of turning 40. "How do you want to celebrate?" her husband, Larry, asked.

"By climbing Kala Pattar."

"Kala Pa What?"

"It's a spur of Pumori. You can see Mount Everest from the summit—much more clearly than from base camp because you're not below her. You're looking across."

"Her?" Larry repeated—dumbfounded, but only momentarily.

"Smee," Larry sighed. (They called each other Smee, after Captain Hook's First Mate in Peter Pan.)

"You are not a hiker. You have never camped. What on earth makes you think you can begin in the Himalaya?"

"Everest—Sagarmatha—invited me," Elizabeth replied.

"I want to go. Besides, it would be rude to decline."

Elizabeth's friends (childhood & adult; grade school through grad school; Southwestern, Southern, Midwestern, & Northeastern), her older sister and in–laws (including and especially the extended family in greater London) reached a consensus so immediate, so deep, and—given their profound differences in politics, religion, ethnicity, skirt length, food preferences, sexual preferences, & biorhythms—so broad as to be featured on the ABC Evening News.

"A 39 year–old woman in Arlington, Massachusetts," Peter Jennings somberly announced, "long known for her headstrong, idiosyncratic behavior, is believed this time to have flipped her curly wig."

Elizabeth's mother, of all people, understood. Evelyn (Mrs. Sam) Alexander had been in a snit for more or less 21 years, ever since her husband died. Of late, however, Evelyn was feeling better. She attributed it to branching out. From Park Cities Baptist Church to Highland Park Methodist. From El Chico's Mexican Restaurant to Raphael's. From the Dallas Civic Opera to Theater Three.

"Elizabeth is branching out. It may be good for her," Evelyn told her astonished son–in–law who had excellent reason to believe that Evelyn would do everything in her power to quash Nepal.

"—Make no mistake," said Evelyn regarding Elizabeth's particular way of branching out, "I do not approve.

"I myself"—Evelyn raised her voice an octave for the finale—"would have no more gone off on a joyride and left my husband for three weeks than I would have flown to the moon."

When she said goodbye to Larry, at Logan Airport, Elizabeth burst into loud, uncontrollable, body–wrenching sobs. It was not the kind of crying that evokes the sympathy of fellow travelers or airline personnel. It was the kind of crying that creates panic—that suggests you are meeting a flight that bursts into flames as it hits the tarmac, killing everyone on board.

In this state, Elizabeth would have agreed to anything.

Larry made one request. "Promise me you will turn back at the first sign of mountain sickness."

"I promise," Elizabeth said.

The Snow Leopard trek to Kala Pattar comprised four American clients: Elizabeth, Will, Mark, and Thom; one sirdar, Ang Chuldim; two sherpas; and a cook. The Americans met for the first time at the Shangri–La Hotel in Kathmandu.

Elizabeth staggered into the lobby—after a 13-hour nap—just as Will was establishing himself as an asshole.

"This isn't a first-class hotel! This isn't a second-class hotel! This isn't even a third-class hotel!" Will spewed at the desk clerk.

Will, who had a crew–cut, was apoplectic because the hotel had no blow dryer.

Mark and Thom approached the shaken desk clerk. Mark asked (gently) if the Shangri–La could wash and dry their clothes. A fifth of Irish Whiskey and a bottle of Armagnac had shattered in transit, pervading everything.

Thom leaned back against the desk, his arms outstretched on the counter. "Hello, hello, hel–LO," he said, spotting Elizabeth.

Elizabeth glared.

"What nice triceps you have," Thom observed. "Let me buy you a drink."

Will's crew–cut fell when he saw the plane (Soviet single–prop, early Brezhnev) that would take them from Kathmandu to Lukla. Elizabeth's curls stood straight on end. Mark and Thom remained calm. They had seen worse. They had met in Vietnam, where Thom ran a MASH unit and Mark flew a helicopter that transported the wounded from the field.

In Lukla, two dzokios joined the party, one the kindest dzokio that you could ever hope to meet—the other a perfect specimen of its progenitors (cow & yak), worst traits combined.

"That animal is evil...evil...evil," Elizabeth, Thom, & Mark observed almost in sync.

"Um–hm, for sure," Chuldim confirmed. "I know that

dzokio all his life. Very bad animal. But very strong."

The evil dzokio snorted at Elizabeth. "I could eat you for breakfast," the dzokio said.

In real life—that is, at home in Massachusetts—Elizabeth would have admired the evil dzokio. He whistled "The Internationale" while he worked. He reminded Chuldim, on an hourly basis, that Marx read Shakespeare's complete oeuvre each year and envisioned a golden era in which the workers of the world would relax and go fishing—although, the dzokio added, one might just as enjoyably lie down in the hay.

In Nepal, however, Elizabeth was doing capitalist in a big way. The dzokio resented her bitterly, profoundly, her especially—he was under all a romantic and believed that women should know better.

Elizabeth sympathized, or thought she did; still, she wanted neither to carry her own duffel nor to be eaten, by the dzokio or anyone else. Thom had volunteered to provide a similar service, which he promised would be the highlight of Elizabeth's 40th year, if not her entire life.

The trail from Phakding to Namche Bazaar was, in the final stretch, so narrow and so steep as kept the evil dzokio focused on his footing. As prevented Will from calculating aloud the worth of his portfolio. As almost finished Elizabeth—knee and brain.

She slept through tea, she slept through dinner, she slept through a meteor shower. She awakened the next morning, still exhausted.

"Aaram garnos," a voice advised. "Please rest."

"Umm, good idea," Elizabeth thought—but there was something even more compelling about the timbre of that voice than its advice.

Elizabeth put on her boots and set off toward the sound. She had gone only about ten feet when her right knee collapsed. It screamed its little cap off.

"Fuck you!" it said.

The outburst was fortuitous. When Elizabeth moved to replace the cap, she saw that she was wearing only hiking boots.

"I thought it felt a little breezy."

"No getting one past you," the kneecap said.

On the second try, Elizabeth (warmer, clothed) ascended a low hill. She looked northeast, in the direction of the voice.

Clear air, blue sky—the sky, though, just a frame. And in the frame, the "land of snow": Himalaya. And right before her eyes, as in a dream, the Everest-Lhotse-Nuptse ridge.

Elizabeth bowed as Ang Chuldim had taught her. "Sagarmatha," she said, "Namaste."

"Kati raamro. Wonderful. You've come."

Elizabeth held her breath. She did not want to cry.

"But I'm so tired," she said, "my knee might fail, don't know how far..." Her voice trailed off, the fog rolled in, the mountains disappeared.

Will, by contrast, felt "tip top" that morning, as he informed Thom and Mark while clambering past them. He ran so far ahead that he got lost in the Gokyo valley, en route to Phortse. In a panic, Will carved his initials into each scant juniper.

Chuldim searched high and higher. Just before sunset, he located Will—who set Chuldim to gathering firewood for a shower.

The evil dzokio saw everything. It enraged him. The dzokio began to look on Will in a way that no one had foreseen.

On the fourth night out, the dzokio ate Will for dinner. It made quite a mess; still, the cook, sherpas, & every other member of the party were delighted.

"Way to go, old boy!" Mark raised a pitcher of chang to the dzokio's lips.

Thom clapped him on the withers.

"Nice work. Take out bad guy," Chuldim agreed.

Elizabeth wondered whether the dzokio's appetite had been satisfied.

Unfortunately, the dzokio failed to observe a cardinal rule of food safety: refrigerate leftovers immediately. To make matters worse, the greedy dzokio indulged in a midnight snack, then polished Will off for breakfast. Soon after he finished, the dzokio bleated at the pain in his head. He quaked as his fever spiked to 104°. His abdomen cramped. His stomachs subdivided. Then it all came out: the dzokio got violently & disgustingly ill.

Thom held the dzokio's head, smoothing his forelock with a blue bandana. Thom reached into his little black bag.

"Better living through chemistry," he said.

But none of Thom's prescription medicines did the trick.

Mark emerged from his tent, uncharacteristically wide-eyed of an early morning. He inhaled luxuriantly—hashish procured in Kathmandu.

"Try this," Mark said. He held the joint for the dzokio, who puffed on it gamely.

"Fol-low the drinking gourd ," the dzokio moaned.

Chuldim rubbed the dzokio's hindquarters.

"You take day off," he said. "Americans carry bags."

When it saw what it was in for, Elizabeth's kneecap had a conniption such as the Eastern world had never seen. The fit was lost on Elizabeth. She unceremoniously popped the kneecap back in place. Elizabeth was listening, intently, to a voice that over several days had risen almost to the surface of her mind. "You promised," said the voice, "at the first sign..."

Through sheer dint of will—his stomachs swirling, head

pounding—the dzokio raised one hoof, then another. Several miles behind the other dzokio, Thom, Mark and Chuldim, the evil dzokio made his way toward Tengboche.

He remained within sight of Elizabeth. As he saw her set off, fall down, massage her knee, take water, tighten her bootlaces, the dzokio softened. He changed his mind.

"That is one plucky dzomo," the dzokio said.

Plucky or not, toward sunset, when she and the dzokio reached Tengboche, Elizabeth was just about done for. She hardly saw the blooming rhododendron, a whole protected forest of it, outside the monastery. She hardly felt the San Miguel that Mark (or Thom) set in her hand.

"I feel... so...tired," Elizabeth said.

"How do you think we all feel?" Thom's actions, though, belied his jocularity.

He covered and uncovered Elizabeth's eyes, one at a time. He shined his headlamp into them—and frowned.

Thom dug into his little black bag. "Take this," he said, "tonight and the next night and the next—until we start down.

"Now," he said, "Let's go to bed."

Elizabeth was not that tired.

"Alright, alright . . . you go to bed."

As Elizabeth nodded off, the voice—Larry's voice—rose again in her mind. This time she heard it clearly. "Smee," it said.

"Come down."

Around midnight, the dzokio raised the flap of Elizabeth's tent with his right hoof.

Elizabeth stirred. Awakened. Stared.

The hoof waved back & forth, beckoning her out.

The dzokio drew Elizabeth toward him, cradling her in the crook of his left foreleg. With his right forefoot, the dzokio dipped a red bandana into a bowl of warm water. He washed Elizabeth's face, patted it dry.

The dzokio lifted Elizabeth onto his back and carried her to the animal pen. He set her gently on a mound of fresh, clean hay.

"Aaram garnos," said the dzokio. "Please rest."

He curled up beside her.

Elizabeth awakened the next morning feeling fit as a fiddle, if with a few loose strings. She attributed the cure not only to Thom's Diamox but also to the dzokio's ministrations.

"Um–hum, for sure. That very good dzokio," Chuldim agreed.

The next stretch, from Tengboche to Loboche, would have been easy but for the gain in altitude from 12,700' to 16,175'. Thom and Mark took their minds off it by imagining what they would eat and drink when they all returned to the Shangri–La Hotel.

"Steak—and I don't mean yak," Thom licked his lips.

"G and Ts in the pool," Mark sighed.

The dzokio had weighed Elizabeth's education in the balance and found it lacking. He took it upon himself to fill the chasms, commencing with a lecture on . . . something that started in medias re.

"Greatest happiness of the greatest number!" the dzokio roared.

"Utilitarianism—" Mark began.

"—Jeremy Bentham!" Elizabeth interrupted.

The dzokio cleared his throat. "This isn't Password," he said dryly.

The dzokio had intended to expound upon the inevitability of mortal decay, using Bentham's corpse—the head entombed in a refrigerated safe at University College—as an example. He was silenced by a look from Ang Chuldim.

The dzokio sulked for several hours. "All right then," he snorted. "Tell me a story."

"Once upon a time," Elizabeth began, "in separate brick houses—one with gray shutters, the other with dark green—lived two little girls named Elizabeth and Anne. They had known each other all their lives, maybe longer."

"Were they good little girls?" asked the dzokio.

"They were mischievous."

Elizabeth told the dzokio how she and Anne, bored with a game called Candyland, had cooked the hot fudge sundae card in Anne's toy oven—hoping to generate an actual hot fudge sundae but setting a small fire instead.

"What happened then?" the dzokio asked.

"The University Park Fire Department came."

Elizabeth's stories of her childhood confirmed all the dzokio's prejudices concerning the irremediable decadence of the American bourgeoisie and the sense of entitlement that they fostered in their offspring.

"Did you have no chores?" the dzokio demanded.

"I made my bed, except on Wednesdays, when Ida changed the sheets."

"It's a good thing that I like you," the dzokio said.

That night the cook prepared a feast to fuel the hike up Kala Pattar. It began with garlic soup and ended with dried cherry cake. It included yak cheese, yak steak, dhal bhaat, and something that once was green.

Thom heaved enormous portions onto Elizabeth's plate.

"Bulk up," he said.

They set off an hour before dawn. China's mountains emerged before them, India's behind in the rising sun.

The dzokio plodded along to 17,000', then ensconced himself at Gorak Shep ("Dead Crow"). He nosed into his saddlebag and, from it, retrieved a cold can of Elizabeth's favorite beverage, a staple of her diet in Massachusetts.

"It's Dr. Pepper time," the dzokio said.

Even Mark and Thom got downright misty-eyed.

The dzokio waved them off with a hoof. He hated prolonged goodbyes.

"Jaane ho. Onward," the dzokio said. "You have nothing to lose but your necks."

They spread themselves along the trail. Chuldim moved in spurts, running ahead, then pausing for the others to catch up. When Elizabeth reached him, Chuldim was smoking a cigarette.

Elizabeth gaped at the cigarette. She could hardly breathe.

Chuldim extinguished the light, pocketed the butt. "Sherpa oxygen," he explained.

In the first half–hour, the mountain came into view.

"Sagarmatha," Elizabeth bowed. "Namaste."

But the only possible sign of recognition that she received was the telltale plume, which trembled in the clear morning air.

Mark extended his arm. He tapped his wrist. The altimeter read "17,700'."

"There are some things," Thom said, "that it is better not to know."

They looked downhill toward Gorak Shep. The dzokio was poised on his hindlegs and holding something rectangular.

Mark reached for his binoculars. “I’ll be damned,” he said.

The dzokio raised a cardboard sign with the letter H. The H became an E, an M, an O, a—

“Hemoglobin,” John read. “Excellent mantra.”

Elizabeth nodded, too winded to speak.

Chuldim stayed behind with her as Mark and Thom went on.

Elizabeth slowed, stumbled, crept—stopped, altogether. She scowled at the scree.

A good 75 vertical feet remained.

“Ee-lizabeth?” asked Chuldim.

“I’m thinking...” Elizabeth said.

She felt a ferocious pulse in her wrists and temples, she heard her heartbeat, the atrial “lub” the ventricular “DUB” that skipped—had always skipped—from time to time.

Elizabeth hatched a plan. She could not walk upright. But she could crawl.

“I’ll follow you,” she told Chuldim. “My hands in your footsteps.”

Chuldim was not wild about this idea, but he agreed.

Some 15 minutes passed. Some 15 billion red blood

cells were born and died. And in those 15 minutes, Elizabeth crawled to the summit of Kala Pattar. She sat down beside a cairn strewn with prayer flags. She looked across the bed of the Khumbu Glacier.

"Remember me," said Sagarmatha. "Namaste."

FORM

David Barringer

The interviewer wanted to know, for the record, how our marriage was.

"Rocky," I said.

"Very rocky," agreed my wife.

"Worse than that," I said.

"Yeah," said my wife, "much worse."

"It's a shambles," I said.

"We're on the outs," she said.

"We're on the skids," I said.

"We're separating," she said.

"Actually," I said, "separation is a fait accompli."

"We've been living separate lives for some time now," she said.

"Years, really," I said.

"Doomed from the start," said my wife.

"It just took this interview process for us to admit what's been staring us in the face," I said.

The interviewer depressed the STOP button. My wife had moved the candles and pepper (no more salt for us) and hand-blown glass bowl from Sweden to make room on the kitchen table for the interviewer's audio recorder. Our recorded interview was to be incorporated as voice-over during our husband-and-wife montage in the video. The interviewer sat back and recrossed his legs. His checklist of questions was on his clipboard, which he now hugged to his chest like a young doctor amused by a smartass patient but ready to deliver his diagnosis about which there could be no foolishness.

"I get you," he said. "You're sick of this. I understand. It's a long process. I know how families get. You're not alone. It's common. I also know you hired me because you truly want a unique, high-quality digital-video card this Christmas. You want your friends and family to know how you're doing, what's going on in your life. You want them to know you care. It's human nature. Since cave persons painted on rocks. Since

Native Americans sent smoke signals. It's also human nature to resist a little, rebel a little. Stick in a caricature on those cave walls. Sneak in a dirty joke in a few extra puffs. I understand. So take some time. I'll work with what I've got so far. I'll give you a day or two for Halloween, then we'll start back fresh, first thing in November." He bagged his recorder, saluted us with his clipboard, and let himself out.

For the past two weeks, we'd grown used to his comings and goings. We'd even given him the password for the home alarm. That was probably stupid of us, my wife and I both agreed, irresponsible of us. His crew would show up to film the morning dash to get out of the house. They filmed my wife at her office for a half-hour one day. My wife had to tell her company sort of the truth, that the guy with the camera was a family friend shooting a holiday video for the grandparents. That seemed to make it okay. They filmed us individually; personal interviews with my daughter in her room, my son in his room, me in my home office, my wife in the kitchen, all so we could say funny things about each other, mock insults, mock confessions, as if they were real. The film schedule for November included a Thanksgiving Day shoot and, a few days later, the big shoot: a shoot on the day the landscape crew would arrive to plant the blue spruce in our backyard and we would go out and chop it down, our whole family leaning into the saw like the soldiers planting the flag at Iwo Jima, and then we would drag the tree inside and, likely enough, get into an argument about whether the tree would be perfectly upright with a little more to the left, a little more to the right, back this way, to me, no, that's too much, back to you, it's still not right, and then Johnny Mathis on the stereo during the family tree-trimming, shimmy-shimmy here, huggy-hug there, candy canes and hot chocolate. That was to be the big shoot. There'd be others but not many because post-production was going to eat up at least a week, and then they had to crank out a hundred DVDs for everyone on our list, and then we had to allow at least three days for mailing so our little holiday form video could arrive before Christmas during the busiest mailing season of the year.

"We're not really a shambles, are we?" asked my wife.

She asked this after we'd sat there a moment smiling at the departed interviewer's reaction to our sarcasm. He probably wasn't more than 22, getting his chops doing Christmas and wedding and anniversary videos one family at a time before launching himself at one of the big firms that contracted with companies to produce the same kind of special-occasion videos for employees and employee families. That was where the big money was.

I leaned over and kissed my wife, nosed her cheeks and inhaled so deeply I suctioned her cheek into my nostril and it stayed stuck there.

"Gross!" she cried. She pulled away, laughing, rubbing at her cheek, looking for a place to wipe it off, then smearing her hand on my shirt, which I let her do, laughing.

"Look at it this way," I said, spreading my arms wide. "We've got two days of freedom."

My wife covered her face and sobbed.

I wasn't prepared for this. She was really sobbing. I was thinking, Oh, shit, what did I miss now?

"Oh, Honey," I said, reaching out to her. I petted her hair and cradled her head and was moving in for the top-of-the-head smooch when she suddenly peeked out. Her face was a jack-o'-lantern of mischievous glee.

"Boo!"

I feigned shock. Some of my shock was sincere. Mostly I felt relief. She was joking. That meant I didn't have to cheer her up, to convince her our marriage was so not a shambles and how much I loved her, etc. Then I felt ashamed. I should embrace this husbandly duty—no, not duty, but privilege, the privilege of loving one's spouse and, almost more importantly, informing her of love's nature and resilience and inestimable duration. "I get you," I said. "That's a good one."

My wife sat back, sinking deeply into her advantage, savoring it. "Why do you love me?" she asked.

I had to think fast here, which sometimes I'm good at, thinking fast, finding a witty remark to defend myself, delaying deep feeling, or at least buying time.

"I'm sorry, Honey," I said, "but I signed a confidentiality agreement with the kid before my interview. You'll have to wait for the movie."

I held my poker face as long as I could, which wasn't all that long. I can't lie to my wife, and she rejoices in that fact.

"Oh, I get you," my wife said. She stood and unbuttoned her shirt and walked out of the kitchen.

I followed.

She headed up the stairs. "I can wait for the movie," said my wife, naked from the waist up, pausing in our bedroom doorway. She licked her own nipple. She actually cupped her breast, lifted it, and flicked her tongue at her own nipple.

Holy shit, I thought. She's never done that before. Well, I mean, in front of me.

"You can wait for the movie, huh?" I asked her.

"Yup," she said.

I followed her into our bedroom.

We undressed and got into bed.

"I love you," I said.

And then I told her everything I would never, in my life, tell some wise-ass kid with a video camera.

FREE BURGERS FOR LIFE

Ryan Boudinot

A few months ago I won a free deluxe cheeseburger, fry and 12 oz. Fountain drink every day for the rest of my life from Big Dave's drive-thru burgers. I often ate there on my lunch breaks when I worked at the print shop next door. The print shop had been surviving on industrial safety manuals and church bulletins for years, but had recently begun branching out into digital photography and web design. Mr. Meyer, my boss, had sunk what was supposed to be his retirement fund into new technology and a series of consultants who fed him contradictory information he didn't understand anyway. He ended up with a scanner that wasn't compatible with his PC, a printer that continually jammed and a bunch of software that was way over our heads. Harlan Meyer got suckered into any offer that involved free promotional merchandise, so all we had to show for our efforts was a storage box full of glare guards, a couple lumbar supports, and mouse pads. Even during the times Mr. Meyer couldn't pay me, I still showed up for work, mostly to mess around on the computer. Being laid off and having a place to hang out like the print shop combined the best aspects of being unemployed and having a job. I could take breaks whenever I wanted and any work I actually performed made Mr. Meyer guilty enough to buy me lunch. So naturally, when Big Dave's announced its Free Burgers for Life contest, I was one of the first to enter. I was even there when they drew the winner one Sunday morning. They had billed it as a big media event, but the only journalist who showed up was Josh Bland, an ex–rock star who wrote a column for the alternative weekly, the one that ran the ads for escort services that I masturbated to when I was drunk.

During the ceremony, Josh Bland sat in the "barnyard," the kids' section furnished with saddles instead of booths, scribbling notes, sipping his complimentary mocha shake and mumbling cryptically into a tape recorder. He basically made fun of everybody in the article.

All the parents and siblings of Big Dave's employees had shown up to receive their free "Family Appreciation Day" meals, even though it was ten in the morning. Dennis, the manager and son of the joint's deceased founder (Dave), passed out kazoos and silly hats and encouraged everyone to wear their 20th Anniversary T-shirt. Dennis' wife, Theresa, remained in the back manning the fry station and telling would-be customers coming through the drive-thru that the place was closed. She had a physical deformity, a harelip, and was shy around anyone outside Big Dave's circle of employees and suppliers. For a long time I thought she was deaf. She refused to speak to me as a customer. Whenever I said hello she'd do a little pinky-wave and go back to restocking napkins.

I usually took my extended lunches at Big Dave's whenever Mr. Meyer's wife Rita showed up unannounced to provoke Mr. Meyer into vicious arguments about money and software. Rita would try to flatter me and belittle her husband in a single sentence. "If you'd just hire more geniuses like Elliott around here, Harlan, then maybe you wouldn't have to subcontract out for Internet whatever-it-is." She was stubbornly Luddite and acted as though she weren't so much uninterested in computers as above them. Maybe this attitude was her way of expressing resentment at Mr. Meyer for squandering their money on what she considered toys. The Meyers had mentioned they were going to show up for the Free Burgers for Life ceremony, but never did.

Dennis had officially invited the public, but there were few of us among the crowd of teenagers and their parents. Somebody called us all over to the condiment bar, where Dennis drew my name from a cardboard box covered in aluminum foil and masking tape. For a second his mouth went slack then pulled itself back up into a wrinkly grin while everyone clapped. I later found out that Dennis and Theresa suspected me of rigging the contest. That evening after closing they opened the ballot box and read all the entries. I had submitted only one. There was no way they could stop me from claiming my prize. Later still, I found out that Big Dave's employees had been encouraged to enter the drawing as many times as they wanted, encouraged, in fact, to fill out stacks of ballots in the break room. Dennis hoped to give the prize to one of the teenagers who worked for him. I was so elated I didn't even notice how disappointed everyone else was.

I'm not usually an extravagant kind of guy. At wedding receptions and bar mitzvahs I'm not known as the kind of dancer who hogs the floor and gets serious for three hours straight. I'm more the kind of dancer who, when called upon, can bust a particular move that shows everyone I am the shit. I have one discernable talent on the dance floor, one maneuver I retained from my grade school gymnastics class. First, I kick my right leg forward and my left leg back, dropping to full splits. Then, without using my hands, I rise back up to a standing position. I then drop to the floor with my left leg forward and my right leg back, and finally rise again to continue dancing like it's no big deal. It's not the move itself that impresses people, but the nonchalance with which I execute it. But that day, after I performed it on Big Dave's freshly waxed brown tile floor, I had a hard time containing myself and kind of hurt my groin.

****

I was entitled to any combination of menu items up to a five-dollar value every day for the rest of my life. If I wanted to substitute a chicken sandwich or a French dip for the burger or a soft-serv cone for the fries, I was welcome to do so. If I wanted four orders of fries, that was no problem. Or five Cokes. If I missed a day, it didn't mean I got two meals the next day. All I had to do was show them my little laminated card which, incidentally, I had laminated personally, as Big Dave's did all their copy work through the print shop. Mostly coupons and fliers. Big Dave's offered forty-seven different flavors of shake and I was determined to try every one of them at least once. All they did to make a new flavor was dump different syrups from the espresso bar into vanilla ice cream and stir it up. Never trust espresso from a burger place, I have found.

About a month after I won the drawing my brother Steve visited me so I took him out for a complimentary burger, fry, and fountain drink. He's twenty years old and goes to a liberal arts college nobody has ever heard of. He's an art major and once sent me, as a Christmas gift, a green mannequin head with a light bulb inside it. He said it was a lamp but there was no way for the light to get out. Steve is the kind of person who watches TV for hours just so he can make fun of it. He has a withering comment for any advertisement, popular band, movie or book that he perceives as pandering to mainstream tastes. Maybe I'm being too harsh. No, not really. I was always the responsible one, he was always the screw-up. He had dreadlocks for a while, I have always had short hair, etc. There are times, though, when I've wondered if he is a genius and I'm a thirty year-old loser making paper clip chains at a string of boring gigs. He has his own website, a mess of penis enlargement ads scanned from porno mags and links that lead you in circles, which I had been checking out at work and finding pretty amusing. We emailed each other every couple weeks and when he dropped me a note to say he was coming into town I held off telling him about my prize because I wanted to see his reaction. He arrived at my apartment in his van, where he lives. Our parents don't approve of it, but I think it's pretty cool actually. He's got a little refrigerator in there, curtains on the windows, and a foldout bed.

On our way to Big Dave's, Steve couldn't stop laughing about my free burgers for life. I hadn't been in his van for a while and the whole thing smelled like cat pee.

"Did you get a cat?" I said.

"Not that I'm aware of," Steve said.

"Has there been a cat in here recently?"

"What are you saying?"

"What is this, old Pink Floyd we're listening to?"

"Velvet. What? Velvet Underground."

"You still got my Creedence CD?"

"You think it smells bad in here or something?"

I could fill the rest of this tale with our back and forth, but we had burgers to eat. It was raining hard when we pulled up to the Big D. A teenage guy with a really thin head named Milo stood in the landscaping, wearing a sandwich board advertising $1.99 double cheeseburgers, waving at traffic hissing past him on the arterial.

"Hey Elliott! How's it going!" Don, Sandra, Dennis, Carlo, Marie, Thomas and Paula greeted me as we entered the building. Theresa, the fake-out deaf-mute, didn't say anything.

"Hi everybody. I brought my brother along with me today."

"Hi, Elliott's brother!"

Steve stood beside me trembling with laughter while I surveyed the menu as though for the first time.

"So what does your heart desire?" I said.

"Elliott, man, I can't believe this. This is so fuckin' great," Steve said.

Steve ordered a garden burger, fries, and a kiwi-almond shake. I paid for a deluxe baked potato, side salad with 1000 Island, and a small pop. We sat in a booth across from some high school girls who had all ordered large Cokes and were busy dabbing droplets of pop on their scrunched up straw wrappers to make them expand.

"See this?" I said, pointing to the specials menu in its plastic standee frame, "I printed this."

"Wow, impressive," Steve said, flipping it around, "Oops. Spotted a typo."

"You're kidding me. Where?"

"Here. Says 'bruger' instead of 'burger.'"

"Damn. How come I didn't catch that?"

Sandra slid our tray onto the table and asked if I had gotten sick of eating here yet. She was one of those proud, overweight black girls you see with the elaborate hairstyles. Her hair today was diagonally cantilevered out over her forehead. I liked her a lot. We'd gotten to talking a few days before about desktop publishing. She was going to a community college, studying graphic arts. I told her that if she wanted to apply at the print shop she could put me down as a reference, even though I knew there was no way Mr. Meyer was ever going to hire more than one employee at a time.

"Whatever you do, stay away from the fishwich," Sandra said.

"Why's that?"

"I'm not at liberty to say. Nondisclosure agreement. We take an oath, raise our right hand and all that shit."

I had sensed a lot of tension in Big Dave's that day, as if everybody was wearing his or her required smile despite some horrible drama that had played out just before we arrived. Steve sat across from me eating his fries in that retarded way he always has, dipping each individual fry into a carefully opened ketchup packet. Every few seconds he'd snort, look around, and shake his head or roll his eyes. It was starting to piss me off. If I was going to share my free food with the guy, I expected a little gratitude.

"You still seeing that one chick, what's her face?" Steve said.

"You talking about Katy?"

"That must be the one."

"No, I'm not. I mean yeah, in a way."

"What the hell is that supposed to mean? Yay or nay?"

"We broke up awhile ago. But we still see each other once in awhile."

"Ah, nostalgia fucking."

"I didn't say that," I said.

"Well, do you call meeting each other for coffee 'still seeing each other?' Still seeing each other means—"

"What about you? Still going out with that girl from Arizona or wherever?"

"Colorado. Dude, I had my first three-way with her and her roommate last week."

Which goes to show how my younger brother's sex life had always been more exotic and fulfilling than my own. I both wanted to hear about it and didn't want to hear about it. Steve recounted the entire incident—the scented oils, the hot wax on nipples—in a perhaps louder-than-necessary voice, causing a booth of elderly women whom I had seen holding hands and praying over their side salads to pick up their trays and move to the other side of the restaurant. The high school girls, on the other hand, expended a great deal of energy pretending not to listen. I knew that if I said anything Steve would make an even bigger show of it, so I decided instead to suffer through the story, stirring chives and bacon bits into my cold potato. Outside, the rain dumped on Milo, who looked increasingly pathetic the more enthusiastically he tried to wave. I felt bad for the guy.

Perhaps this was punishment for something he had done to the fishwiches.

I scribbled some numbers on a napkin, figuring out how much my free meals were costing Big Dave's. Five dollars times 365 days was $1,825. Granted, there were days when I didn't reach my five-dollar limit and a couple days when I didn't get anything at all, but my prize was costing them at least $1,500 a year. Take away the markup, which I guessed to be about fifty percent, and my free burgers, fries, and pops were setting them back about $750. Which is probably about as much as Big Dave's made on a good day.

"You think this place can really afford to give me a free meal every day for the rest of my life?" I said.

Steve shook his head. "The whole thing has the vibe of a last-gasp promotional deal to me. I wouldn't be surprised if this place went out of business soon."

****

Most of the time after work I got my food from the drive-thru, then went home and ate it alone in my apartment. I have never had a weight problem, owing it to my high metabolism. But after a few weeks I started noticing a ring around my belly like a slowly inflating inner tube. For breakfast

I usually ate toast and for lunch a couple of those instant soups you just pour hot water into. On a couple occasions I threw up after eating my barbecue burger or chicken fillet. My body was telling me it was tired of Big Dave's but I couldn't resist my free meal. I enjoyed getting something for free, whether or not I really wanted it. Once I even took a single bite out of a double bacon cheeseburger and stuffed the rest down the garbage disposal with a spatula.

****

I decided one night to shop for a birthday card for Katy, who hadn't returned my calls for a month. I thought she would budge a little if I got her something sweet, one of those cards with a poem in it or a funny cartoon. I was in Hallmark when Sandra snuck up behind me and pinched me on the neck.

"You don't work at Big Dave's anymore," I said, "Where did you go?"

"I got a new job! Last week, at the Nickel and Dime Want-Ads. I'm gonna be doing layout and paste-up. You still getting those free burgers? Damn, Elliott. I thought you would have gotten mad cow disease by now."

"Free food is free food, I guess. Who's the lucky person?"

Sandra was holding a teddy bear crammed into a coffee mug.

"It's for my nephew, James. He turns three this weekend."

"Your nephew drinks coffee?"

"Oh, say Elliott. I'm glad I ran into you. You still showing up on Milo's shift?"

"Yeah, once in awhile."

Sandra looked concerned. It took her awhile to communicate through euphemisms and gestures what Milo had done that I should be aware of. Not only had he been spitting into my burgers, but he put a pube in one of them.

I felt it was my responsibility to report Milo to Dennis. We sat in the booth furthest from the counter and I recounted what I had been told. Dennis shook his head and breathed a lot through his nose and rubbed his mustache. He still wore his drive-thru headset and microphone.

"Did you find some, uh, evidence in one of your burgers?" Dennis said.

"An inside source told me."

"It was Sandra, wasn't it?"

"Well, yeah."

Dennis rolled his eyes. "Sandra got fired last week. She had some bone to pick with Milo. I'm sure she just lied to get him in trouble. We caught her on surveillance cam stealing chicken patties from the walk-in. She's been diagnosed as a pathological liar and now she's in therapy for it."

"You're kidding. She seems so cool."

"Oh, she's a great kid. No question. She's just a kleptomaniac and has some problems comprehending the truth. She was stealing from the tampon machine for Christsakes. When we confronted her with the chicken patty thing, she denied it, even when we played her footage from the cam. She said it was doctored, that we had this big conspiracy against her because she's black. Really severe pathological liars like Sandra believe their own lies, even when the facts are staring them straight in the face. I've been doing a little research about this stuff online. I'm sure Sandra believes in her heart that what she told you was true. She probably thinks you're a nice guy and wants you to like her. But basically she has this self-esteem problem. She loves attention. People listen to her when she makes up some big story. She probably told you she's going to Community College, right?"

I nodded, sadly.

"Well it isn't true. She picks up things from talk shows and goes with them, steals other peoples' psychodramas and reenacts them for your sympathy. It's really pretty sad. At any rate, I'm sorry she upset you. Tell you what. I have to get back to the drive thru. Want a couple burgers?"

****

I drove around the parking lot of the grocery store where Katy worked trying to watch her through the windows. There were signs advertising two-for-one maple bars and 99-cent canned peaches in the way, but I could see her at the express lane checking people out. If I drove by the front of the store at about three miles–per–hour I could see her for maybe five seconds. She had her hair up in a ponytail and was wearing the red vest the store illegally made their employees pay for. I used to pick her up when she was working swing shift and she'd give me free day-old donuts from the bakery. I wanted to marry Katy and move to Alaska. I've never actually been to Alaska, but Steve has and I've seen pictures of the place. The sun shines 24-7 up there during the summer. But there's a downside, the winter, when all you can do is drink and plot your suicide. Then everything gets better again. Katy hadn't written or called me since I sent her that card. I had even added a couple lines to the poem myself.

I watched another checker walk up to Katy and say something, gesturing out the window. Katy turned and saw me. I gunned it and stared straight ahead, as if I was on my way someplace else.

****

Some of the print jobs Mr. Meyer took on were just bizarre. End-of-the-world propaganda and UPC symbol = 666 type stuff. I'd seen a lot of right–wing literature come through that I didn't particularly agree with, but when you're in the print business you have to leave your political views at the door. Besides, he was paying me $6.50 an hour and I didn't particularly care where it was coming from.

I came to work one Monday to find Mr. Meyer sitting at my desk, dividing all my papers into little piles. His stringy hair was combed over his bald spot, except for a few strands that stuck straight up off the side of his head like a flag on a mailbox. I could tell he'd been here awhile, working himself up for something.

"Mr. Meyer. You're sitting in my chair."

"I think we have to talk, Elliott."

"Okay."

"I'd like to know the meaning of this," he said, sliding some printouts across the desk.

"They're my brother's website."

"Your brother is quite an artist."

"I think so."

"Besides the fact there's a rule here about using the

equipment and supplies for personal use, I don't approve of my computer being used to download pornography."

"Pornography?"

"Take a look."

I flipped through the pile of paper. Reviews of shows, angry commentary about oil companies, poorly drawn pothead comics. Then I found what Mr. Meyer must have been talking about."

"You're kidding. It's just a drawing. It's not even a photo."

"Smut is smut, whether it is drawn or not."

"But it's not like he's advocating bestiality."

It was hopeless. Mr. Meyer was the boss and I was the employee. He would have laid me off again sooner or later anyway. Truthfully, I had been walking the edge for months now. Typos weren't the half of it. Steve's website was just the reason he found for finally getting around to firing me.

****

A double cheeseburger with no tomatoes, a large curly fry, and a small chocolate peanut–butter shake. Side of ranch for the fries, please. Yes, I'm aware that's twenty-five cents extra.

****

That night Tony, Miguel, and Lissa visited me at my apartment. They're high school kids I occasionally buy beer for. Once in awhile they give me a free CD. Miguel works at a music store and gets to take home the promos. That's how I've kept up with current music. They let me keep the change whenever I buy for them. Usually it's just a couple half racks. When they came over I was in rough shape, watching Taxi reruns in my sweat pants, smoking some cigarettes Steve accidentally left at my place. Miguel put a new disc on the stereo. Lissa laid on the couch with her head in Tony's lap, groaning, "I'm so tired," while Tony provided a running commentary on kids dropping acid in a shop class and science–fiction movies. Tony had grown a mustache before it was actually thick enough to look like he wasn't trying so hard to grow one. Truth is, I saw something of myself in Tony and perhaps that's why I kept agreeing to buy for them. I was amused by their company. Plus, free CDs.

"Then this really fat chick was fuckin' all like…"

"What kind of beer do you guys want?" I finally said.

"You all right, Elliott? You seem kinda burnt," Lissa said. If only I was ten years younger, as they say. She was making me horny the way she was draped all over Tony, who seemed not to notice or care. High school sex. In playgrounds at night, in parents' bedrooms. Katy had still been in high school when we had begun dating the year before, but she had been a senior. Lissa was a sophomore. She could have passed for a senior, though.

"I got fired today."

"Sounds like we need to treat you tonight, my friend," Tony said, though I knew he didn't really consider me a friend.

"Whatever you guys want. Let's just get it over with. What'll it be?"

Tony slid a couple twenties across the coffee table with the toe of his elaborate basketball shoe. "We'll go for a couple racks of the fancier shit tonight. You pick it out. Plus a couple forties."

"I'll be right back, then," I said, putting on my jacket. The apartment complex is next door to a mini mart. Within five minutes I had returned with their beer and some change.

"You guys can drink it here if you want," I said. The stereo was playing something I didn't understand, something that didn't sound like music but like a bunch of photocopiers and barking dogs with a woman saying the same thing over and over again. Tony commandeered the remote and cracked the first beer. I used to have cable but forgot to pay the bill for a few months so now all I had left were the local channels.

"Can I use your bathroom?" Lissa said.

"Yeah, sure," I said, trying to visualize the sorry state of my toilet bowl. I shivered, thinking of what Milo had done to my burger. I felt embarrassed but also a little aroused by the idea that Lissa was using my bathroom. I used to watch Katy pee after we had sex. I tried to pass it off as just curiosity, but I think toward the end she suspected it was more than that. Once I even told her to pee on me in the shower, but then pretended I'd been joking when she flipped out about it. Katy wasn't what you'd call sexually adventurous. She had three things she did and that was about it. Not like I imagined Lissa to be. Damn, if only I was in high school . She was one of those slightly plump girls I find so attractive for whatever reason. And if only Tony wasn't in the picture. I hoped he'd leave or pass out so I could mess around with her. Then there was Miguel to think about. No matter how much he drank, he never seemed to get drunk. He just sat in a corner with his hat pulled over his eyes, pretending to scratch records on an imaginary turntable.

"Still getting them free burgers?" Tony said.

"Still going strong," I said, cracking another beer.

"Dude, maybe we should rent a movie," Tony said.

"I've got a lot of movies here. They're in that milk crate under the T-shirt."

While Tony dug through my DVDs I pretended to look for something in my bedroom so I could "accidentally" run into

Lissa. I heard her washing her hands and arranged to be coming out of the bedroom as she was leaving the bathroom. She gave a little embarrassed smile and said "Hi," then turned toward the living room.

"Hey, hold on," I said, "I wanted to ask you something. I wanted to know if you guys knew where I could get some pot."

"Tony's the one to ask."

"I just thought you might know."

"We could probably get some for you. Tony knows these guys." Lissa started toward the other room and shouted to Tony over the music, "Hey Tony, know where Elliott can score some bud?"

"Elliott! The man!" Tony laughed.

They made a big show out of it but I wasn't really after pot at all. I just wanted to get high with Lissa alone in my bedroom. I drank two more beers and put on the director's cut of Blade Runner. Miguel mumbled something about a Spanish exchange student who had a lot of bud on him and was willing to give it away to make friends with Americans. We all crammed into my car, with Tony and Lissa groping in the back and Miguel manipulating the EQ on my crappy stereo in the front. We drove past the bowling alley and the espresso huts and all those places where you can get an oil change and I thought about Katy in her red vest running cans of vegetables over the scanner, except in my daydream the scanner didn't pick up the bar code and she had to run the same can over the laser again and again, stubbornly refusing to manually type in the code. She never wanted to see the movies I wanted to see, never wanted to go to a new restaurant or try a new menu item at Denny's where we usually went on our dates. She refused to give me head. She threw a shit fit if she missed Everybody Loves Raymond because she hadn't missed an episode since the series began. Why couldn't I stop thinking about her? Every time I called, her parents erased my messages, I was sure. Her dad even answered a couple times and told me to stop calling and even though I was respectful of him he still wouldn't let me talk to her. On our way to get the pot we drove past the grocery store where she worked, but I didn't see her car in the parking lot, which was strange because her shift was right now. Maybe she had gone home sick. I wondered if I should call her to make sure she was all right.

Ferdinand, the guy we were going to get the pot from, lived with the Andersons, his host family, in one of the yuppier neighborhoods in the hills above where I lived. Tony said it would probably look bad if I came along, so I parked a block away and sat in the car while he and Miguel went to see if he was home. Lissa laid down in the back seat.

"You can sit in the front, you know. You don't have to make me feel like a chauffeur."

Lissa sat up and rested her chin on the back of my seat and started blowing on my neck to annoy me but you know what it really did. I couldn't believe it. Knowing I was supposed to tell her to knock it off, I gave her hand a slap. I also knew this would get her to do it more and she did. She laughed and fell back in her seat and said, "I think I just got my period."

"Did you need something right away?" I said, trying to sound sensitive to her womanly needs, "I think I have some old Dunkin Donuts napkins in the glove box."

"Um, let me see," she said. I could hear her sticking her hand down the front of her pants, the actual scratchiness of her pubic hair. She checked her fingers. I tried to look in the rear view mirror but it was too dark and she was lying down. I think she saw me looking. "Yeah, I think that would be a good idea," she said.

I opened the glove compartment and grabbed a handful of thin little pink and orange napkins. I heard her unzip her jeans and shove them into her underwear.

"You're not going to tell Tony about this, are you? He'll make fun of me," she said.

"No, of course not," I said, "Why are you going out with a guy like Tony, anyway? You could do so much better than him."

"What, you think he's a dick?"

"I didn't say that."

"Yeah, you did. You think he's a loser. Well guess what, Mr. Elliott. He's talented. You should see the sculptures he does in wood shop. He's not half the loser you are."

That really hurt. I cranked the radio, which was playing the kind of music I listened to in high school, good music, none of this electronic crap. Boston, Grand Funk, Bachman Turner Overdrive. I wanted to turn around and slap Lissa but Miguel, Tony and Ferdinand had already returned.

"Pleased to meet you," Ferdinand said as he squeezed into the back. "You want pot? I get you the kind of pot that gets you so stoned."

Ferdinand didn't know his way around town very well, and if her did, he wasn't giving very good directions. Besides, Tony kept messing him up asking how to say certain obscenities in Spanish, which struck me as odd because Miguel spoke Spanish and Tony could have asked him. With Miguel translating Ferdinand's directions, we ended up in the parking lot at the mall. Ferdinand disappeared into a Starbucks and started talking to one of the baristas. This suddenly felt volatile to me, entrusting a drug deal to a high school student who had only lived here a month and didn't speak any English. I put the car in gear and got out of there.

"Hey! What are you doing! Stop, you fuckin' prick!"

As soon as I got to the first light, Tony, Miguel, and Lissa all bailed out of the car. Tony flipped me off and spit on my windshield, called me something he'd just learned. I hated those kids anyway. We'd see next week when they came back begging me to buy for them again.

I was still feeling hungry and decided to get some more food at Big Dave's. I pulled up to the drive-thru, where Dennis was working.

"Didn't you already get your free meal today?" Dennis said, leaning out of the window.

"Yeah, but I thought maybe I could get tomorrow's meal in advance," I said, "I promise not to come back tomorrow."

"That's not the way it works. Have you been drinking?"

"Come on, man. It's just a burger, fries, and soft drink. OK, forget the fries. It's not like I'm going to rip you off. What difference does it make whether I get tomorrow's free burger today?"

"You're putting me in an uncomfortable position, Elliott."

"You mean you're not going to give it to me? Come on."

"Sorry."

"Asshole," I said, and drove away.

Back at home I did up a packet of beef-flavored Ramen and started crying. There was a message from Judy in the rental office saying I was behind on rent. I called Katy again but no answer. Now I really did want some pot and felt bad that I had left those kids all the way out at the strip mall without a car. I was pissed off at Steve for no good reason so I called him but he wasn't home or wasn't answering. I left three messages on his voicemail, the first one angry, the second one apologetic, the third one crying, asking him to come over because I was in really bad shape. I overcooked the Ramen and tried to breathe as I ate the noodles while the TV played episodes of shows I liked when I was in grade school. The kids had left their beer and I decided I was going to drink all fifteen that were left, plus the lone forty that sat perspiring on the kitchen counter. I decided to watch the entire Star Wars trilogy with headphones on. I fell asleep before Luke and Obi-Wan even make it to Mos Eisley.

****

I wasn't going to take this avoidance from Katy anymore, was my first thought when I woke up. I needed some orange juice and a good meal, I decided, but I had left the bread bag open and there were only two stale heels left. In order to conserve orange juice, I made a glass at a time, taking a spoon full of concentrate from a can in the freezer and mixing it in a glass of water. I decided to not overly dilute my OJ this morning and treated myself to three glasses, after which I threw up. I ate a couple Oreos, put my clothes on and drove to the grocery store. I saw Katy's car in the parking lot and entered through the deli entrance so she wouldn't see me. She was working the express again. I pretended I was shopping, picking out a couple things, a potato, some Cream of Wheat, a bottle of soy sauce. She must have seen me because suddenly another checker was working her lane. I asked her where Katy was. She said she didn't know, that Katy had just gone on break. I could tell the checker was covering for her and besides, the morning shift had just started so it wasn't time for Katy's break yet. My head felt like it was being repeatedly slammed in a pair of automatic doors. I went back to the employee bathrooms, knowing that's where she went when she didn't want to see me, and waited for her to come out. When she did, she jumped and gave me this awful look.

"What's going on? Why don't you return my calls?" I said, "Didn't you get the card I sent you? With the—the poem I added to?" I followed her through the store. Shoppers were looking but I didn't care.

"Leave. I want you to leave."

"I'm shopping just like everyone else. I have a right to shop here," I said, holding up my potato.

"I can get a restraining order, you know."

"You think I'm some kind of stalker? What is this? You

didn't even congratulate me on winning the contest. Free burgers for life. For life. You know what that means? I can take you out any time you want. You can even get something over the five dollar value and I'll pay the difference."

Somebody tapped me on the shoulder. Why do all white, male, middle-aged grocers look the same? He asked me to get out. I told him I had some things to buy. He let me pay at checkstand 8, where a woman I had never seen before scanned my items and put them in a plastic bag. I had forgotten my checkbook and I'd left the change from the beer on the coffee table, so I tried to use my debit card but found I had insufficient funds. Katy had disappeared again, probably to go cry somewhere. I didn't want that food anyway.

****

By the time my hangover disappeared, I decided I needed to get a new job. I only had a few hundred in savings and that was all going to get sucked up in rent. I decided to place a "Help Available!" ad in the Nickel and Dime, because that's how I got my job at the print shop. I drove out to the little office complex and was surprised when I walked into the suite to find Sandra sitting behind the reception desk. I think she was surprised to see me, too, or maybe I just looked like crap. I stammered a little and finally told her everything Dennis had said about her. She shook her head and fumed.

"That asshole had it out for me ever since I started working there. He treats all his employees of color like that. He's the pathological liar. Milo really did do that to your burger."

I was so angry I forgot why I was there to begin with. Finally I calmed down enough to dictate her an ad and pay the twenty-dollar fee with a check. I could transfer money later to cover it, but I would end up forgetting and the check would bounce anyway.

I drove to Big Dave's to find both Milo and Dennis working. I was starving, so I ordered first and just stewed until my order came up.

"I didn't appreciate what you pulled last night," Dennis said as he handed me my bag.

"And I didn't appreciate being lied to, prick."

"Whoa. Whoa there," Dennis said.

"I saw Sandra today at the Nickel and Dime Want Ads. She works there, like she said. She didn't fucking lie about it. I don't understand how you can make such a big deal about your fucking contest, the we-love-our-customers bit and then turn around and treat the winner with such disrespect. You!" I pointed to Milo, who stood nervously with a mop in his hand next to the fry baskets, "You're gonna get sued you twisted son of a bitch."

There were people looking. I was so tired of people looking. A table full of little girls having a birthday party started to cry. Some big guy with ketchup on his chin helped Dennis push me out the door, but I didn't budge until I noticed the strip of tape running alongside the door marking off increments of feet. Remembering the security cam, I bolted.

On my way home I ran out of gas and had to park in the bowling alley parking lot. It was only a block from my apartment, so I just walked. What made me most irate was that I had left my free food on the counter; I hadn't grabbed it while being forcibly removed. Now they were sure to revoke my free burgers for life, I just knew it, and I started to cry again.

At home I finally yanked my picture of Katy out of its frame, tore it into pieces and flushed them down the toilet. It was the portrait she had posed for at Glamour Shots, where they spend two hours coordinating your outfit and doing your makeup for you. I got her that for Christmas. When my toaster burnt my bread heels even on its lowest setting, I yanked it out of the wall and threw it on the floor. I would have destroyed a lot more stuff if Steve hadn't showed up.

"What the fuck is this?" he said from the doorway. My free burger days were over, I realized. If only I had known that a month later Dennis and Theresa would torch the place in a sad attempt at insurance fraud, I would have been happier. I told Steve that I didn't really blame him for getting me fired, that I'd had it coming. I had accidentally exposed four hundred dollars worth of photographic paper, had shown up for work late on several occasions and had misplaced some negatives for an important client, so we had to schedule a reshoot. I had inadvertently erased files from the computer, left the coffee maker on overnight and spilled toner on the masters of the Rotary Club Annual Report. Steve put his arm around me and asked if I was hungry, which made me cry harder. He'd take me out to lunch, he said.

"I have no friends in this town anymore," I said, "How come it's so hard to get people to like me?"

Steve took me to Royal Fork Buffet. I piled my tray with tacos, pizza, salad and four different kinds of dessert. The pizza was too hot to eat but I was starving and I burnt the roof of my mouth. Outside, a tour bus parked and disgorged a group of twenty or so pairs of elderly identical twins. Each pair wore matching hats and windbreakers with nametags. When their took their places in line the whole restaurant stopped eating to gawk at them, but after the novelty wore off and the twins had sat down to eat, nobody seemed to notice them anymore except Steve and me. We watched two old ladies take turns devouring a sundae with a single pair of dentures between them. The one on the left took a bite, removed the dentures, licked them off, then handed them to her sister, who stuck them in her mouth and repeated the process. Steve and I were laughing so hard soda was dribbling out our noses. I tried to imagine what it must be like to grow up knowing someone else that intimately, to wear matching outfits, to finish their sentences for them, to sense their presence across great distances.

MIDGET IN A SUITCASE

Susannah Breslin

i

When the midget daughter turned eighteen, she turned to her full-sized mother, who was sitting next to her on the front seat of the rusting Oldsmobile Cutlass they had lived in for over a year at that point, and she said, “I am going to Hollywood to become a porn star.”

The mother did not turn her head towards her daughter when her daughter said this. Instead, the mother sat staring straight ahead, her hands wrapped tightly around the car’s steering wheel, even though the car wasn’t moving, hadn’t, in fact, moved in months.

The problem, of course, was that the mother was a full-sized person, and the daughter, on the other hand, was a midget. This meant whatever the daughter said—whether it was how hard it was to find pants that fit or how difficult it was to reach high shelves with short limbs—the mother never understood what it was the daughter was talking about.

"Fine," the mother said to the horizon lying on the other side of the windshield.

"Goodbye," the midget told her mother. And, with that, the midget got out of the car, for what in all likelihood would be the very last time, dragging her big suitcase behind her.

ii

When the midget who wanted to become a porn star stepped off the Greyhound bus in Hollywood, a tall man was standing there waiting for her, looking expectantly at her.

"You know," the man told her, as he bent down to breathe hard and fast onto the top of her head, "They do not call me a suitcase-pimp for nothing."

Then, he took the big suitcase out of the midget's small hand and drove her over the hills to Porn Valley.

There, the midget girl climbed up a long flight of stairs to a second-floor office above a busy intersection. A man who looked like he had wrestled with alligators in the South when he was young shook the midget's hand up and down and showed her all the shiny gold teeth in his mouth. After that, he struggled to lower the tripod for his camera.

The midget girl, for her part, stood naked against the wood-paneled wall, her hands spread out in embarrassment like chubby starfishes over her small boobs and even smaller nipples. The camera, for its part, popped and flashed her into a white oblivion.

iii

By the time the midget girl woke up the next day in a hotel room, the phone was already ringing. "Yes," she told a man. She would have sex today for three hundred dollars.

At noon, she was lying on her back on a bed on a soundstage, waiting for the camera's lens to come out from behind its lens cap and her co-star's penis to un-hide itself from behind its zipper. She worked hard, as best she could, in this manner for the rest of the day.

After several weeks, the midget porn star lost track of the number of men's names she had stored away in the tiny cubbyholes of her mind, and she no longer had the ability to remember the amount of dollar bills she had tucked into her suitcase, and she could not recall how many small roles she had in the many movies at the local adult video store.

After several months, the midget porn star found herself stepping out onto a large stage in a big Las Vegas casino, wearing a miniature ball gown that had been custom cut to reveal her tiny cleavage. She had won Best Actress in a Specialty Video. She stood on her tiptoes to reach the microphone and told the people gathered there, “Thank you.”

Even though the full-sized porn starlets on adult movie sets still sometimes bumped her in the head with their bony knees and even though her male co-stars occasionally still had to be taken aside to be told exactly how to do things with her, now she was famous.

Someday, the midget porn star decided, it was possible that her mother would come across a magazine rack with her daughter’s face on it, and maybe at some point between the time her mother bit her tongue in surprise and peered quietly at the photos in the privacy of the Cutlass, for one second, her mother would be proud. It was possible.

iv

One year passed.

Every morning, the midget porn star watched her giant TV in her sprawling condominium.

Every night, she remembered that even though her body was and always would be small, her life, such as it was, was filled to overflowing with a dumpster's worth of sadness.

After all, there was no one in this world with whom she could truly see eye-to-eye.

Everyone wanted to dress her up like a miniature Zombie or a dancing Tinkerbell.

No one wanted her to star in a one-on-one adult video with a man her own size.

Every day, when she woke up once more, her dreams were all long gone.

v

Finally, when she could not take it any longer, the midget porn star bought herself a plane ticket to take her back to the town where she had lived in the car with her mother.

The day she arrived, a taxi picked her up at the airport. From there, she went to Toys 'R' Us. She spent a long time in the aisle where the cars for children were parked.

After much consideration, she decided on the shiny black one with the red racing stripe.

So, out of the store's parking lot in the tiny car she drove.

Down the twisting back alleyways of her hometown, she took left turns and right turns until she was back on the same street where she had lived in the car with her mother.

Of course, her mother was still there.

Now, her mother was passed out on a dirty mattress next to a listing, urine-stained cardboard tee-pee. The Oldsmobile was nowhere to be found.

vi

The midget daughter waited in her small car just around the corner from her sleeping mother, thinking about everything that had ever happened to her here in this tiny town.

When twilight came, under the darkening blue sky, she spun the little car out fast and hard around the corner, all at once. Awakened by the high hum of the miniature car's straining battery, the midget's mother sat up suddenly. As her daughter raced toward her, at the last moment, her mother screamed, "You will never hurt me with your small car!"

In fact, the small car did bounce off the mother on the first pass.

But by the time the daughter had finished rolling the little car back and forth over the mother, it appeared the mother had nothing else at all to say.

vii

Two days later, the police called the midget porn star to tell her that her

mother was dead. She told the police that she didn't know if her mother would prefer being jammed into the dirt or burned up in a stove, but when she did, she would let them know.

viii

Two years later, the midget porn star was sitting inside her huge mansion.

She sat on the edge of her enormous bed, swinging her feet back and forth
over the edge.

The only thing she could hear was the sound of her own whistling, blowing
through the empty rooms.

The telephone rang.

"Hello?" the midget said to the telephone.

"Hello," a tiny voice said.

"Come quickly," it told her.

And, so, she did.

ix

When the midget porn star arrived at the address she had been given over the telephone, she found a deserted and overgrown house set back behind a dark
and ivy-covered gate.

Through the gate's bars, she could see a small playhouse

in the front yard.

She squeezed herself between the bars, and walked across the grass to the
playhouse.

Slowly, she opened up the tiny door.

Inside, she found the smallest porn movie set she had ever seen.

Midget filmmakers milled about toting tiny video cameras on their little shoulders. Overhead, a sound-boom hung down in small-scale. The set decorations, it appeared, had been made for those who were small and in porn.

The midget daughter of the dead mother walked in through the door to the middle of the room, and she stood there, in the tiny spotlight, on the world's smallest porn set. A hush fell over the crowd around her as her face lit up with the glow of a small smile.

Then, she took off all her clothes, until, at last, she stood truly naked before the world.

And, as the dark lens of the camera's eye pushed into her, and the midget man of her dreams' manhood rose before her, the midget porn star fell back onto the small bed behind her, so, in this small world, she swooned, realizing that while she had spent much of her life zipped into a big suitcase, she could now leave that luggage behind her.

FLOATING

Richard P. Goodwin

The sign said HALF OFF MASKS. Lester had passed the old novelty shop hundreds of times on his way to and from the office but had never gone inside. He stared in the window at the rows of rubber masks—monsters, aliens, movie stars, politicians. Traffic splashed by in the rain. It was five-thirty but already dark out. Closing his umbrella, Lester went inside.

The man sitting behind the counter looked up from his newspaper but didn't say anything. Sweating under his raincoat, Lester inched about the small, cramped shop, unsure of why he was there. He looked at the games and gags, the plastic guns and clown makeup, the vampire fangs, the colorful wigs. There were more masks at the back of the shop, lined up on a dusty shelf. Lester noticed the rubber head of a horse. It had a furry brown mane and big teeth, crazy bulging eyes.

"Try it on?" came the man's voice. He stepped out from behind the counter, tucking his shirt into his wrinkled trousers. He had a fleshy neck and his head was bald except for some white fuzz at the sides.

"No, thanks."

"Go on and try it," the man said. Reaching up, he took the horse mask off the shelf. He pulled out the cardboard support. "Here."

Why had I come into this place? Lester asked himself. He took the mask and stretched it over his head. It hugged the back of his skull and had a sharp chemical smell. He had to look through the nostrils to see himself in the mirror. He laughed. It was ridiculous.

"Twenty dollars," the man said.

Lester moved his head this way and that. "I don't know," he said, his voice sounding funny.

"That's going down from forty."

Lester studied himself in the mirror a few more moments, then pulled the mask off and smoothed back his thinning blond hair. "You going out of business or something?"

"Fifteen and the horse is yours," the man said.

***

Lester sat at the dining room table, sipping a drink. On his lap, hidden under the tablecloth, was the horse mask. He hadn't shown it to his wife yet. Janine was in the kitchen making dinner.

Listening to the clangs of pots and pans, Lester ran his fingers over the horse's mane. He took a swig of his drink. Then he put the mask on. When Janine came in with the plates, Lester said, "Hello, there."

"What in the god's name?"

Lester didn't say anything. He had to tilt his head back to see her.

"Lester?"

"I bought it," he said.

"Why?" She set the plates on the table and stood looking at him.

"I don't know. It was spontaneous."

"I don't understand."

"I can't say that I understand, either," he said.

"Well, take it off, please. It's hideous. And it's time to eat."

He lifted the mask off and set it on the table. The open mouth looked like it was laughing. The mask was goofy yet somehow sinister, Lester thought. Unbelievable he'd buy such a thing.

"Can you take it off the table, please?" Janine said. "What's gotten into you, Lester?"

He put the mask on the chair beside him. Taking up his knife and fork, he cut into his chicken cutlet.

Over dinner Janine complained about her job, as she had done almost every night for the past month. She hated her co-workers and her boss. She hated the fact that her office had no windows, no air conditioning. She hated the hours she worked and the money she made. There was nothing, absolutely nothing, she liked about being the billing manager of a printing house. Why hadn't she gotten into something else? Art or music or drama or writing. Wouldn't it be nice if she could paint paintings all day or write poetry? People who did that had to be the luckiest in the world.

"I'm sorry I'm laying all this on you," Janine said. "You've probably had a tough day yourself."

"It wasn't so bad," Lester said, and it wasn't. He didn't hate his job, but he couldn't say that he liked it, either. It was just something he did each day without pain or joy, frustration or reward. He sold life insurance.

"I wish I knew what to do."

"Quit," Lester said.

"I can't do that, Lester."

"Yes, you can," Lester said. Then he put on the horse mask. "You can do anything you want."

"Lester, take that off. We're eating dinner. What is wrong with you?"

Carefully Lester forked a string bean through the open mouth of the mask. He chewed, watching his wife's face go from anger to confusion to a kind of horror. "Okay, I'll take it off," he said.

***

"This isn't funny anymore," Janine said later that night. She'd just gotten out of the shower and was wrapped in a towel, standing at the foot of the bed.

Lester lifted his head from the pillow. Through the nostrils of the mask he looked at his wife's cleavage, her thighs. "Mr. Horse wants you to come to bed," he said. "Mr. Horse wants you to fuck the daylights out of him." He made a neighing sound. He was naked except for the mask, and he could feel himself getting aroused.

"Knock it off," Janine snapped. She came over and

ripped the mask from his head and flung it to the floor. "Stupid grotesque thing. I hate it."

Lester watched as Janine removed her towel and slipped into bed. When she shut out the light, he nestled up to her and said, "I'm sorry."

"I can't understand you."

He kissed her face, her neck, massaging her belly with his fingers. "I know, I know. I'm sorry."

"Don't put that stupid thing on again."

"I won't," he said, and climbed on top of her.

***

The next morning Lester came to breakfast wearing the mask. He was dressed in a dark blue suit, striped tie and wingtip shoes. Janine was pouring coffee. She just looked at him.

Lester said, "Mr. Horse is hungry."

The toaster popped. Janine tossed the slices on two plates and set out butter and jam. She sat down and spooned cream and sugar into her coffee.

"Doesn't Mr. Horse get a good morning?" Lester said, moving closer to her. He picked up his coffee and considered drinking it through the mask. But he'd burn himself and ruin his suit, he thought. He made a whinnying sound.

"Keep playing your little games, Lester," Janine said finally. "See where they get you."

Lester took the mask off. His face was red, his hair tossed about. "What is it?"

She didn't answer him.

"What's the matter?"

"You're being a complete idiot," Janine said.

After breakfast they left the apartment together and walked in silence toward the train station. Passing the novelty shop, Lester looked in the window at the masks. The half-price sign was still there, but the shop hadn't opened yet. He wanted to tell Janine that this was where he'd bought the horse, but he kept quiet. He knew she didn't want to hear about it.

They said goodbye on the concourse. Lester watched Janine hurry toward the southbound platform. Suddenly he wanted to run after her and apologize for the prank he'd played at breakfast. She really was stirred up by this, wasn't she? He ought to go and give her a big hug. But then he'd miss his train and be late to work. There was a lot to do today.

Lester turned and headed for the northbound platform, where the train was due to leave in two minutes. In his briefcase, packed in with his files and reports and sack lunch, was the horse mask.

***

Sitting in his cubicle, chewing on his thumbnail, Lester stared at the phone unit on the desk. He had a load of calls to make that morning but couldn't bring himself to take up the receiver, as if the phone were a bomb that would blow him to pieces. He just sat there, feeling strange, like he was floating inside himself. For the past few weeks he'd been having this sensation but hadn't told anyone about it. Like he was two people, one inside the other, and the inner one was trying to get out. He looked at his briefcase on the floor.

All around him the salespeople were busy at their jobs—hustling on the phone, pecking at their keyboards, punching up figures on their calculators. "Oh I can take care of that for you, no problem, sir," Lester heard Ned Rogerson say in the next cubicle. Ned kept a bottle of Rumplemintz in the toilet tank of the men's room. Lester had caught him one day slipping the lid off the tank.

Ned poked his head over the divider. "Awfully quiet over here," he said. He had watery eyes and a red nose. Recently he'd colored his hair black to hide the gray.

"I'm waiting for a call," Lester said.

Resting his arms on the edge of the divider, Ned said, "How about a drink tonight?"

"No, not tonight." Lester gnawed on his thumbnail.

"What's up?'

"Nothing's up," Lester said. Damn he felt weird. Swimming inside his own body was the only way he'd be able to describe it.

"Tomorrow night?"

"I don't know. Maybe."

Ned sank back into his cubicle.

Taking up his briefcase, Lester headed across the bright, noisy office to the men's room. He closed himself in the last stall, sat on the toilet and put on the horse mask. On the stall door someone had written I SOLD MY SOUL FOR THIS MISERABLE HELLHOLE. Lester breathed deep. He knew this was odd—hiding in the toilet in a mask—but he didn't move. He liked the way the mask felt, he had to admit.

Someone came into the men's room. Lester listened. Sweat trickled down his scalp and his heart began to thud. The urinal flushed, then the person washed and dried his hands and went out the door. Lester let out a breath, as if he had narrowly missed being caught. Caught doing what? Was he doing anything wrong? Could he get fired for wearing a horse mask in the restroom? He realized he didn't care if they fired him. It didn't matter if he worked here another fifty years or if he left tomorrow, or in five minutes. It was just a job.

That was Janine's problem. She expected too much from her work. She expected to come home each day feeling elated, like she'd changed the world. She wasn't going to change the world. Lester would have to tell her that next time she started up with her bitching.

He got to his feet and lifted the lid off the toilet tank, removed the bottle from inside and unscrewed the cap. Through the mouth of the mask he took a drink of Rumplemintz. It was very sweet. His gut became warm. He took five good pulls on the bottle, floating inside the ocean of his body.

The men's room door opened. Quietly Lester put the bottle in the tank and replaced the lid. He crouched to look under the stall, recognizing Ned's worn brown loafers and floodwater slacks. As Ned stood in front of the urinal, Lester came out of the stall.

He gave a long neigh.

Ned jerked around, urine sprinkling the floor. "Jesus!"

"It's me, Ned. It's Lester."

"What the hell are you doing?" He finished his business and punched the flusher.

"I'm a horse," Lester said.

"I can see that. Halloween's not for, what, another seven months?"

Lester whinnied and blew air past his lips. He began

scraping his shoe across the tiles.

"Wow," Ned said with a laugh. "Crazy."

"Do you have any oats?" Lester said. He knew he should stop this now, take off the mask and end this foolishness and get back to his desk. But he kept going. "Horses love oats and I want some oats. Where can I get some oats in this hellhole? I'd sell my soul for some oats."

"God damn, Les, you've gone bonkers. Keep guard, will you, Trigger?" He brushed past Lester into the stall to get the Rumplemintz. He studied the level a moment, then shrugged and had a long swallow. Holding the bottle out to Lester, he said, "Quick."

Lester shook his head, blowing air through his lips.

"Suit yourself," Ned said and had another long drink.

***

On his way to the station after work, rain misting down out of the dark sky, Lester stopped at the novelty shop to ask if they carried any other horse masks. He thought it would be good to have a couple different ones lying around the house, one in his desk drawer at the office. The owner didn't seem to remember him.

"I bought that mask that was right up there," Lester said,

pointing to the space on the shelf. The shop was empty and quiet.

"Oh, you," the man said. He ran a hand over his bald head. "Okay, you're the horse guy."

"Do you have any others? Any different horses?"

"No."

"Are you sure?"

"Would I lie?"

Lester looked at the other masks. He undid a button on his raincoat. Somewhere out in the city a siren wailed.

"How about Humphrey Bogart?" the man said. "Or a ghoul. Would you like to be a ghoul?"

"I want to be a horse," Lester said. "Maybe a Shetland pony."

"I can't help you there," the man said.

Lester thanked him and left.

He caught the express and then walked the three blocks to his apartment building. Standing outside the entrance, he looked up at the fourth floor. The lights were on—Janine was already home. Lester closed his umbrella, mist beading on his pale thin face. He wondered if he should put the mask on now or when he got inside. He decided to wait until he got inside.

Lester stepped off the elevator and walked down the dim corridor toward his apartment. Behind someone's door a baby was crying. Before fitting the key into his own door, Lester stretched the mask over his head. He was about to turn the lock when he withdrew the key and put it in his pocket. He knocked on the door. It would be better to surprise her this way. Mr. Horse was paying her a little visit. Mr. Horse was making a house call. He covered the peephole with his finger.

"Who is it?" came Janine's voice.

"It's me," Lester said. "It's Lester."

"Why can't I see you?"

"Just open the door," he said.

She opened the door. Lester scraped his shoe on the floor and forced air through his lips. He neighed, shaking his head violently.

Janine's hand went to her mouth.

"Mr. Horse wants to come in," Lester said.

The door slammed. The deadbolt clicked.

Lester knocked, waited. He knocked again. Then he opened the door with his key and went inside.

"Janny?" Lester tilted his head back to see down the hall, the horse's mane sticking out from the collar of his raincoat. A sizzling sound came from the kitchen. "Hey, Janny?"

She didn't answer.

In the kitchen Lester turned down the flame under a skillet of pork chops, which had begun to burn. Water was boiling in a pot on another burner, dripping over the sides. Sweat streamed down Lester's face under the mask. He tasted salt on his lips. He went to the bedroom.

The door was closed but not locked. Poking his head inside, he said in a soft voice, "Janny." She was in bed, buried under the covers. Lester could see that she was shaking. Then he realized she was crying.

A sad feeling opened in him. He wanted to take off the mask, but he didn't. He wanted to stop this, but something pushed him on. He went over to the bed and laid a hand on his wife's trembling side. "Mr. Horse doesn't mean any harm," he said.

She was crying with force now. The expression "letting it all out" came to Lester. This probably wasn't just about the mask. This had something to do with her job, too, and other things they hadn't discussed. Maybe a lot of things. She was having some problems right now, he understood. She was under pressure. He patted her side and said, "It's okay. Everything's going to be okay." He knelt down beside the bed.

Slowly she turned to look at him. Seeing the gaping mouth of the mask, the wide nostrils and pointy ears, Janine screamed and pulled the covers over herself. "Get away from me!"

"Let it all out," Lester said.

"Lester, please just leave. Oh god, please leave me be."

Tears washed down her face.

He stood and peeled off the mask, looking around the room. “There,” he said, “I took it off.”

But she was still crying.

***

“How ‘bout that drink tonight?” Ned said, leaning over the divider. His eyes were glazed and red. It was four-o’clock. Phones were ringing all over the office. People scurried about under the fluorescent lights.

“Yeah, sure, whatever,” Lester said. The night before, Janine had threatened to call the police if he came home after work today. “Stay the hell out,” she’d said. “I don’t want you in this apartment.” Of course he would come home after work—it was his apartment, too—but he figured he’d give her some time to cool down. Let her think things over. He’d show up around eight or nine tonight, with a card or some flowers—not wearing the mask, of course—and everything would be all right.

At five o’clock, Lester shut down his computer and began tidying his desk, realizing he hadn’t done a single productive thing all day. He hadn’t sold any policies or found any new clients or returned the calls of his current clients. He’d just sat there, feeling like his chair was lifting him toward the ceiling. A few times he'd gone into the men's room to put on the horse mask and drink some of Ned's Rumplemintz.

It was raining again. Ned didn't have an umbrella, so Lester had to keep them both dry with his as they made their way to the bar. Lester didn't like being so close to Ned, rubbing shoulders with him, smelling him, but they would be at the bar soon enough, he told himself, where they'd get a big booth and sit far apart from each other.

Stepping into the dark bar, Lester imagined himself wearing the horse mask, neighing and kicking his feet and shaking his head, as everyone stared in amazement. Some would laugh. Others would make jokes. Still others wouldn't know what to say. It would be an electric moment. He would feel powerful.

They slid into a booth and ordered cocktails. As they clicked glasses, Ned said, "Here's to life insurance. May they all die with their heads up their asses."

Lester wasn't sure what he meant, but he didn't question it. He drank his drink. From the time he'd gotten up that morning the floating sensation had not left him. He glanced at his briefcase.

"You haven't been getting a helluva lot done, lately, I notice," Ned said with a laugh, his head bobbing on his scrawny shoulders.

You are human garbage, Lester thought. Suddenly he saw himself reaching across the table and raking his fingers down Ned's face. "I'm working some things out," Lester said.

"You never really did explain that deal in the bathroom yesterday. Wearing that horse head. What the hell was that all about?"

"It wasn't about anything."

"Just felt like dressing up like a horse in the toilet, huh?"

Lester looked around the room and sipped his drink. He was floating up out of his body, through the top of his skull, up and up. He breathed, trying to settle himself.

"Hey, Les, earth to Lester," Ned said.

"What is it?"

"Don't worry." He touched his glass to Lester's. "I won't tell anybody about your horse if you don't tell about my little...you know."

Without a word Lester stood, grabbed his briefcase and headed across the bar. He went past the men's room and down the hall toward the glowing exit sign. Ramming the door open, he found himself standing in an alley, the rain coming down on him. He looked around at the rusty metal barrels, the milk crates, the trash, the oily puddles dotted by the rain.

Setting his briefcase on a Dumpster, he took out the mask and fit it over his head. He left the case open, the rain pelting his documents, which he hadn't looked at in days, weeks. Staring down the dark, wet alley, he scraped his shoe across the pavement once and then twice. He pushed air past his lips and made a whinnying noise and began shaking his head around, scraping his foot again and again.

Then the back door shot open and Ned came out. "Lester?"

Lester swung his fist against the side of Ned's head. Ned flew off his feet and landed with a crash in a crate of empty cans and bottles. Lifting one of the metal barrels high in the air, Lester looked down at the salesman sprawled in the rain. He neighed angrily. A beer can rolled across the alley.

Ned's eyes opened wide as the man in the horse mask brought the barrel down on top of him.

CAP'N COOK'S: THE LOST MEMO

Dan Kennedy

FOREWARD:

There are a handful of these memos in the archives at *mcsweeneys.net*. The idea was that they were issued by this character who managed a corporate seafood place and had to address his employees regularly with these newsletter memo things. And at a certain point, me and the other parties involved all kind of agreed that it was time for the character to move on. And so he did. But quite a while after these pieces had stopped running on *McSweeney's*, I found one on my computer and realized that The Cap'n had indeed departed with his legacy in tact by leaving behind one last dispatch that fell between the cracks and never made its way into the world. It was left behind in the shuffle of having all agreed that it was time for The Cap'n to sail off into the sunset. The Lost Memo, if you will. A never-before seen missive that painted the picture of a tired and aging seafood chain restaurant manager locked in a losing battle with his employee's loyalty to Hip Hop culture. This is that lost memo.

—Dan Kennedy, New York, Winter 2003.

CAP'N COOK'S: THE LOST MEMO:

ATTENTION, PEOPLE: THE CAP'N ORDERS ALL, "WE ARE NOT RUNNING A HIP HOP SHIP."

The next person who alters the feedback forms on tables that read "Help us make sure we run our ship in tip-top shape" to read "Help us make shit on our hip hop ship" will be terminated, mateys. No two ways about mutiny. Those cards are on our tables so that people might give us feedback on how we can better serve on the high seas of the rather competitive waterfront food vending business. If you deface the signs, customers are less likely to bother filling out the form. Especially when the message you convey in the altered text is negative or purposefully intimidating (Ahoy! First Mate Ty Lopez! It has not gone unnoticed that cards in your section have been defaced to read, "Help us run from Captain Shit". If you want to deface property and do grafitti, then good luck finding the Hip Hop ship that is manned by Captain Shit…I hope they have as flexible schedules, competitive wages, and fair discounts to employees. In the meantime, when you're on board my boat/franchise (Store 3398) I expect you to fly a regulation customer feedback flag and sail by my rules.

RECCOMENDING MENU ITEMS TO GUESTS

ACCEPTABLE:

–"I have tried those, and I really like them!"

–"Well, if you can keep a secret…the [name of item] is a personal favorite of The Cap'n himself!"

–"Aye! The [menu items] are a fine lot, Matey!"

ABSOLUTELY UNACCEPTABLE:

–"If you need more time, I'll come back."

–Saying nothing or looking away, acting like you did not hear the guest ask about item.

–"I freak that sh** like I'm trying to have a baby with it." (Note #2 to Mr. Lopez: you will be visited an Undercover Secret Spy Cap'n ® at an undisclosed date who will sit in your section and report back to me. Translation to your language: Keep it clean, Coolio. Or: The fuzz is here, junior. Surprise Mr. Lopez, I was young once, too. I know all the jive/slang/wrap/hootie/blowfish/tick -tock/crap/ding dong/ private dick lingo)

BIRTHDAY SONG REMINDER

We have had certain First Mates and Galley Supervisors insisting on jazzing up the birthday song with unapproved lyrics. IN NO CIRCUMSTANCES ARE YOU TO SING THE FOLLOWING SUBSTITUTE LINES AT ANY POINT DURING YOUR TABLE SIDE PERFORMANCE:

–"Jeff admits he is gay."

–"It's your Birthday, G. And if you're ballin' let me hear you say 'Aiiiight!'"

–"The kitchen closes in ten minutes"

LASTLY, HAVE A GOOD SUMMER

It makes the Cap'n weep in his barrel of rum that this has to be the LAST message in the log. It should certainly be the first, but unfortunately we've got some bad apples on board. Some apples that came from South America and are rotten and bruised. An apple that could ripen to be a great apple like the others in the barrel if he would only do some work on himself and ripen up a bit. An apple that doesn't realize he is more valuable as a fresh and ripe apple as opposed to the fermented soft spot he is becoming and even thought apples don't write rude hip hop graffiti about people, the apple I'm talking about reminds me of Ty Lopez quite a lot. I hope that the rest of the barrel realizes they are apples who remind me of the rest of the people on our Pirate Staff and that I hope those apples/staff members can hang in there while we wait on one single apple/person to get with the program. In case you are wondering, I am not actually talking about apples at all, folks. The "apples" are a Pirate Staff that I hope can hang in there. Have a good summer!

Ahoy! Ahoy! Ahoy!
Say it again for summer!
Ahoy! Ahoy! Ahoy!

A LOVE STORY

Josh Kron

In a clear plastic bag: There is[1] a photograph[2]. In this photograph are two people; a girl[3] and a boy[4], eighteen years of age, perhaps twenty, perhaps a couple, perhaps siblings. They are white-Caucasian, though their physical features suggest they belong to different ethnic persuasions. In the picture, their arms—his right, her left—are

[1] The only aspect of this photograph retaining the present tense 3rd

interlocking onto each other's far shoulder, his plush peach palm[5] resting on her sloping skin. When looking[6] at the photograph at an angle perpendicular to its alignment, the girl appears on the left side, and the boy on the right. She is sitting upright in her chair[7], while he is leaning back in a way that says I am cool[8], thus her left arm stays parallel to the ground, until it curves behind his neck and hooks onto his chest. Her left hand (when facing the direction in which they are looking) is in a fist.[9] As noted earlier in the text, the boy is leaning back into the chair, and his head is tilted severely to his right, towards her, so that it resides on

---

person conjunction of 'to be' is the material it is printed on, and the chemicals in the ink, which creates the image. All the contents and subjects within the photograph are long deceased, destroyed, dissolved, and forgotten.

[2] Entered in as evidence by Officer Kobe H. Peres, numbered code *SB.HAF.081106.A*

[3] She was named Anna by her parents, the name originating from Scandinavian/Northern German descent. In the photograph she is eighteen years old. She has a twin sister, though not identical, who is not present in the photograph. She is leaving for university the day after the photograph is taken. She was born on the 8th of a cold December, in a cold 1984. She died on the 15th of a warm May in 2005, in Cape Cod, in a car crash, about two years before she was to graduate, eight years before she was to receive a PhD in something impressive, nine years before her first marriage, and ten years before she was to have her first child.

[4] Noah prefers to be referred to as a man, having had is Bar Mitzvah almost a full six years, at Beth Am, the People's Temple, where he had

a fifty-degree angle. This causes his neck to look unusually large and slightly strained, and shows off a well-defined facial bone structure. There are the beginnings of a beard on the lower grades of his cheeks, and clusters on his chin.[10] The boy is wearing a tight white t-shirt, which really has no business fitting him at all. On it, large red print, is DyNAMO, and in smaller black print bellow it, Soccer Club of New Jersey.[11] There is a red exclamation point; his face is European, Jewish, perhaps Ashkenazi. His ears, ripples and folds of skin, caves of cartilage, stick out a little too far, grow a little too large, lobes are a little too long. He is not smiling in the picture, but he looks serious and informed, and tough. His lips are pale but soft[12], and his eyes are gorgeous. His eyes are green and are gorgeous,

---

a crush on Samantha Ralphowitz when he was twelve, prior to the production of this photograph. The name derives itself from biblical times, from the infamous sailor who built an ark and saved the world, his mother, reclining in a wicker rocking chair, would tell him. Noah has a sister, younger, and back at home while this moment is being captured. He was born in late November, a valentine's child, and this always disgusted him, because it was a constant and irreversible reminder. He died in a terrorist attack in the northern regions of Israel, near Nahariya, when he was twenty-two; with a bomb he detonated. He left no notes.

[5] She would hold them during the winter, in the beginning, when it was still new and exciting, and the past hadn't even begun yet. A cold winter, but little snow. As it happens to be, the only night it snowed that winter was on their first date, though neither would recognize it as such. They had seen a movie; Monster's Ball, in which a vivid and thrilling sex scene takes place, and Noah is uncomfortable. He doesn't know

with long tendril lashes and dark linear sweeping arching brows, but his eyes have no happiness in them, and are red from the camera. They are looking into it with an astute glare.[13]

She is beautiful.[14] In every way, every dimension and trimension, she is beautiful. Her eyes are soft, brown.[15] Everything about her face is rounded, everything is curved,

---

where to look, can't look at the screen, she can't see that he's enjoying it, but he sees her blushing, in the darkness of the cinema, and he is falling for her fast. It is snowing when they get out, most romantic, *the only night of the year*, and they throw snowballs at fellow pedestrians, and she screams with her mouth open and runs to catch up with him as he is now being chased by an older couple, and she turns the corner and grabs him by the shoulders, and her left thumb so slightly brushes against the back of his neck, and it feels like eternity. She didn't hold his hand that night, but the dates continue (although never called such things) and it gets colder, and on the way to Washington Square Park (where they always go to) she says, my hands are cold, he says, mine are warm, and she doesn't look at him, but with so much courage, slides her hand into his coat pocket, and he is pleased and she is nervous and he closes his plush peach palm around hers, and squeezes it slightly.

[6] He can't believe this. He hasn't worn these jeans in years, preferring the strict dress code of his new faith. But today he's the bomber, *his turn*, his chance for glory, and of course he has to dress accordingly, like a normal plain old Israeli. So the jeans, the one's he forgot about, and when he sits down on the bus, checking to see if he's got everything all in order, he feels something in the back pocket. Dirtied, weathered, faded, but preserved, this photograph, from another time and place, from a boy's past. And he really can't believe it, *he still has it*. And it's not that it's bringing back memories, as he stares into the

she has no angles, the antithesis of trigonometric theory. She is sand, blown into molten glass in the midst of a sweeping wind, the calm of the waves after a storm. She smiles a vulnerable smile, a smile that makes her seem as if she is on the brink of tears and dread and horrific things might happen to her[16]. She can be ruptured too easily. Her smile shows a legion of straight ivory teeth[17]. She is sitting as upright as possible, but appears to be a little too tall for this, so she slouches unhealthily from her chest up—Her chest is not well endowed. Her skin is tanned, from a summer at the beach, and retains the pigment most closely related to that of the intersection of wheat, light khaki, and peachpuff[18]. Her hair is a light brown, and it is straight in the photograph, and it hangs shyly down to the bottom of her neck[19], and covers one of her ears, her right ear. She is wearing a tank top with miniscule horizontal stripes

---

girl's face, but it's bringing back something.

[7] The front passenger seat is fully reclined and it's the funniest thing in the world! Where's my head, what? Oh there it is, ah, what a night, that shit is great, he was gorgeous, oh shut up you slut, *you* slut! How slow are we going? I don't know, it says full. Well speed up then! Use that fuel! How many did you take? I took three, was that too much? Oh, babe, that's not enough at all. Oh, my whole face feels like sex, touch me, just tap my arm, yeah, ah wow that's great, he was in me for so long, amazing, I love this. Hey, talk to the trees, it will be fun, the pines are such gossip queens, my god, ugh, oh wow, the stars, look at them, no, look at the road, no fuck that, it's too beautiful, look at the stars, like deep sea fish, flashlights under ice, look at the milky way, it's like god just came, come on, there's no one there, just look up for a second,

alternating between sea blue and white.[20] On each side of the tank top, is a (cute) silk blue bow where the mainland material meets the straps of the outfit. She is looking into the camera as if everything is okay. Maybe it is.[21]

They are sitting on light wooden chairs of exquisitely simple, post modern, post art deco, post a lot of things design[22]. Much like the girl, the chairs are in a war against the sharp angles, and consist only of soft and smooth and subtle changes to their slope at any given point, with a derivative impossible to calculate. To the left of the girl's head, is a fantastically complex menagerie of flora, sprouting plants of a multitude of hues and species.[23] Picture this; below the bridge of arms, in between the two inner sides of each body, and above the crests of the wooden chairs, a fragment of a Tempstar central

---

for just a second…

[8] He had worked for this image tirelessly, long hours after school in the mirror, studying past photographs, *how long can he keep a straight face?* He wants to look like he doesn't care a about a thing in the world, because he cares so much. He cares about everything. He cares about Anna, and even about her sister, and he cares about what she is thinking *at this very moment*, and he cares about why she cries over homework, because it seems like such a silly thing to cry over, and he cares that she's leaving tomorrow to go away, away from him, even though he has already been away for a year, and he held the relationship together, and now she is leaving, like she has the right to *lead her own life*. He cares that his mother is going to miss him, and he cares that his grandmother might not be alive for much longer. He cares about Anna's mother, and her terminal illness. He cares about the sun and the moon, the high tides and low tides of the shores; he cares about the Middle East peace

cooling appliance. The photograph is taken at nightfall, and was certainly the product of a flash[24].

On the back of the photograph, written in a black ink *Stylus*, ball pointpen[25], is the date 8/20/03.

---

process, and about globalization.

[9] She does this when she's nervous, and when she is about to freak out, and Noah finds it completely enchanting and endearing. It is one of those subtle nuances, quirky utterances of genetic coding, which he has fallen in love with, *the little things*, and she's nervous now, because photographs are the boundaries of history, because something is changing, they are taken for a reason, she knows, because these times won't be revisited.

[10] He can't help thinking that *that* is a perfect beard. Perfect. For 2003 Noah at least. Totally even, completely graded and shaded. He looks like a champ. And his skin is so clear, and look how youthful he is. He was beautiful, my god, he was handsome. And he's so proud, on that bus, he wants to forget about the woman that he's about to kill and lean over to her and say, *look! Look at this! Look at me! Look how I grand I was!* like he's looking at his son all grown up. The pride of the creator. He can't wait for that—but then he realizes, *I'm never going to be a father, I'm never going to be a daddy.* He's never going to have a son. And for a moment there is a weak bitterness inside of him. And he asks the photograph, he asks Anna, *do you think we would have been good parents? Would you say yes? Just look at us.* She would if she'd look at them. Just look at them. Stars. Noah and Anna, Anna and Noah, each one a disyllable helix, with arms outstretched towards each other, laced fingers gripping, their bodies twisting around and around. DNA. A natural chain reaction.

[11] He teased her to no end for this obvious flaw in her social standing, *the armpit of America*, and this was an essential actor in his rotation of flirtatious conversation starters, walking up behind her in the hall, never looking at her, but poking her slightly in the back as he walks past

---

with some of his buddies and remarks, *Hey New Jersey*, and one day after theater rehersal she says, you know, you don't knock something you haven't tried, and he is taken back by her aggressiveness and he pretends not to care but says yes, and he keeps coming back and Hoboken really isn't so bad, not as bad as he thought.

[12] Behind these lips is a perfect row of teeth, which before the eight years and $6000 in orthodontics, were crooked and unevenly spaced apart. If ones look carefully, the third tooth to the left, from the left middle tooth, is gray, because the nerve has died. It was late February, the day they first kissed. Central Park, and it is cold, but he picks her up from SAT tutoring, and walk amidst the swirling—Do you remember that winter, the one after the 11th, it is surprisingly warm at some points, and this is one of those days, and the caraseoul is open in the park, and he is refusing to ride on it, *I gave those up when I was six*, but she insists. Afterwards, they are walking down 5th Avenue, towards the Plaza, and he spins around to face her and grabs a hold of her right arm, tightly gripping it, *I know a great place*, and she walks, and he runs, and he purchases two chocolate truffles, *I want to show you something*. They are by the fountain, nativity surrounded by tourism; he loves these parts of the city—and he turns his head up to the sky, pauses for a moment and she is curious and excited, and he pulls his right arm back as far as possible, and releases it, like a slingshot, and the truffle—*woosh, swish*—high into the blue, and it hangs 100 feet in the air, *I'm really good at this*, and she watches as he follows the shadow with his mouth slipping open, running back and forth over previous footsteps, calculating velocity, integrals and derivatives, height and mass and gravity, and she is smiling, and the truffle lands wholly into his mouth, into the lower left cheek pocket, and he closes his mouth, and smiles a full smile. But there is a trickling rivulet of red at the corner now, and the eyebrows contort, and she looks in horror, and then amusement, and then humor, as he opens up and he is gushing, terribly. Delirious with joy, she runs into the nearest building and returns with a fist full of paper towels, and she lightly and affectionately dabs and dabs again,

---

until he is all dry, and they are so close to each other now, and they are both just waiting for it to happen.

[15]You'll see this same glare on the back page of the New York Post. It's the same glare, *that* glare, it's there already, showing signs, hints, a shadow of it's future self. Big ideas start small. That glare, like the one you see on the face of Atta after the 11th. The glare of having seen something. He's seen little boys shot by Israeli rockets, he's seen the starvation and humiliation of an entire people. He's seen the refugee camps; he's seen the poverty of hope in old men. He's seen the ugly, artificial, ruthless individualism of the West, and he's seen the gentle, selfless, romantic sacred poems of a faith. The glare of disaster, of something gone terribly wrong, the glare of an anger that can never be understood, the glare of hurt, the glare of something, which was once so beautiful. At one point or another, everyone was beautiful. Hitler had wanted to be a painter.

[14] Mom and dad, cousins, her friends all standing around in the living room, smiling wearily. Candles lit, old home videos playing on the VCR, her favorite CD on the stereo, people talking about the good times, when she scabbed her knee in 1st grade, her first boyfriend, cards to her and her parents on the dresser, next to her favorite belongings; a rolled up movie poster, an old album, a first pair of sneakers, a stuffed animal; the iconography of her youth. Mourners in the corner tearing slightly, just shaking their heads. *You were missed, Anna.* Charlotte set it all up, she was a true friend. Many people came, all for her, but someone didn't show. And he's thinking of her now, wondering why he never came home. And he wants to say sorry to her for this, a thousand times.

[15] On the bus trying to explain. His last confessional: The whys the hows the whens. Time's running out, he's almost at Pat Junction, and soon he's going to have to end it all, but for now he stares. That picture frustrating him, that photograph making him think. And he begins to understand. When he looks into her eyes, it's just so obvious, so simple.

Things were never going to be the same, he can see. In her eyes, its all too clear. That was the end, nothing after it. No closing lines, no credits, no outtakes. No deleted scenes. Those he saves for his fantasies. For rainy days.

But her eyes haven't seen anything, those virgin eyes. He tries to reason with her, tries to prove himself a man. He doesn't want her thinking he did this for no reason. He has reasons. Oh, he's got reasons. She has no idea what his eyes have seen, and what hers haven't. Poverty, poverty, poverty. A little boy hunched over, crouching close to the ground, seeing his father shot to death by IDF. Watching his body ripple, face caving in, fall to the dirt, foot twitching. Just a big slab chunk of meat. Running to the body, hitting it, squeezing it, calling to him, *Abb, Abb*, burying his little face into his father's stomach. Weeping. Old women being kicked out of their homes, young Arab students being arrested for nothing. An entire nation on the streets, begging only for a home. Walls of religious apartheid. And that little boy, still pulling at his father's shirt, screaming at him, anything, trying to understand why his dad won't respond.

There is a war on, doesn't she know? It's a fight for freedom, and he's going to help win it. He can feel their pain. He can feel that little boys tears, and he can see his mother, the father's wife, at home, boiling water for dinner, having no idea that her husband is never coming back. He's never coming home. All of this he has seen, and he wonders why she never did.

[16] Horrible things *will* happen to her, the driver will be drunk, and she will never get a chance to say everything she has been planning to say. Horrible things will happen, she will never see him again after this night, this is the last time, and neither have the slightest clue, she thinks its only temporary. *Why?* She *is* almost always on the brink of tears. She cries over homework, over her mother and father, she cries over him, over his writing, she cries over his departure a year earlier, she will cry over her own, *she is crying right now*, and she wonders why no one can see it.

[17] It is barely noticeable in this photograph, but this invisible Achilles' heal is the source of many hours of teasing, *out of love*, from him, and her mother says, it builds character, Anna, and she says, yea, *its my flaw.* A runaway tooth, wanted for many charges, warrants for its arrest, it must be brought back to its rightful place in front of the left molar, dead or alive. He calls it the extra tooth, and he makes her laugh about it and fall in love with him for it. He brings it up at the dinner table, and she will smile so wide, showing all of them off, and picture this; as if there is a sparkling twinkle on that extra tooth, like a TV commercial to show something shiny and clean, and she will raise her brows and turn her head to and fro to show the entire table, *look at this,* and he will laugh—

[18] She can't tell if it's night or day, it feels warm though; she's a little hot. It's getting brighter, stuffier; she wants to cool off, won't someone crack the window, just a bit? Maybe Noah can get her a glass of water, with some ice in it, it's summer after all, and there's only so much she can do when she is sweating. Is he back already? She thought he would be gone for good. Her skin feels so wet, is it the spilled beer, or his tongue? Someone is screaming in the distance. It feels nice, though, it must be him, or maybe Trevor, the boy she met at the party, he was gorgeous. Why is he being so aggressive? He must have missed her so, she thinks. It's been years since he has kissed her like this, with such passion. They are rolling over. A door opens and she rolls onto grass.

Perhaps he is going to make love to her now; perhaps he will hold her like this all night long. It's hard for her to breathe, she can't really see, but it's turning rather dark, and a voice can be heard. A man is talking to her, she's being strapped to something, lights are flashing, people are yelling, crying. Can't they keep it down? Can't they whisper? She just wants to hold him in silence. It's been a long year. She's been busy with class and stress and exams, can't she just kiss him quietly for a little longer? For just a little longer?

[19] Her hair goes through a terrible crisis the day before he graduates from high school. *It sounded okay*, she says of a botched and horrific experience with a modeling scout. *It was funny, because they have gone after me before*, but Noah isn't laughing, as he is staring at her, shaking his head, and tells her, alright Shaggy, go find Scooby Doo, and she puts her hand on her waist, and he says, come on Steven Tyler, let's just go upstairs. *Bangs*, an experience gone wrong. She had been picked up at a clothing store, and although she has been down this path before, she takes the wrong turn again. They say they will giver her one free hair styling and then they can just take some photos, and Noah says, beware of anything free. After his graduation, they are sitting outside of a loft which is holding a party for the seniors, and is talking to her mom, with her head deeply embedded in her lap, tears streaming down her cheeks, and he is shaking his head again, twirling his finger around her amputated hair, and he loves her so much.

[20] Shadowboxing around memories. The firsts: the first word, walk, and rollercoaster ride. The first kiss, the first love. And her. Her lasts. These are the natural thoughts of a dying man. These are the things that keep him up at night. To know everything. To know every last little thing; what she was wearing, what she was thinking. Not because it matters, but for the details. Even in her death, his selfishness cannot be hidden. They are about to share an experience, and he wants to be there, listening to her panting breathes in the cold air. He wants to see her bleeding from the corners of her lips, and he wants to see her hurt.

He misses her too much to not know everything. And he pleads to her on that bus, *tell me you understand.* That the heat she felt was really his fingers, that the gasoline was his sweat, that yes, she was right, he *had* come back to her, that he was right there next to her. That she shouldn't doubt it for a second, those weren't flames at tall, they were him, all of him, every him. That he was all around her. *Believe.* That it was 2001 Noah kissing her neck, and 2002 Noah whispering into her ear. That it was 2003 Noah's hot breath that caused her to sweat, not a fire, 2004 Noah's fingers wrapped tightly around the small of her back, squeezing her, molding her, shaping her. That it was 2005 Noah that she was calling to, whimpering to, moaning to, and he was listening, standing close by. And it was 1984 Josh holding your hand, his little fist clamped firmly to your pinky, watching over your, burning as well, crying and dying with you, always with you, from the very beginning to the very end.

[21] It was, at some point it was, at some point it was great, on the roof under the stars, in New Jersey on the water front, at the park, on the promenade, the dinners with his family and the dinners with hers, the nights at the movies in Pavonia/Newport, at the ghetto theater, where everyone always screams to the characters on the screen, the smell of the PATH station, the smell of his hair, the days spent walking around with nowhere to go, the days lying in bed with nothing needed to be said, the *American Greetings* internet cards, the online scrabble games. It was good, even the fights were delicious eruptions of emotion otherwise suppressed beneath the layers of pride and stubbornness. The trips to the ocean, the seltzer fights, and she would be cold and wet in her clothing, and he would be laughing hysterically, and she would be furious, and there it is, in that freeze frame, everything you ever wanted to know about the universe.

[22] They bought them in Denmark, for her mom and dad. They spent all day walking through Copenhagen, getting lost, in the constellations of

---

side streets and shops. They end up in a small park, surrounding some castle, and there is this pond. They sit there, for what, two hours maybe, just watching tourists, and Swans, and passersby. This is earlier that summer, the one before she goes to college, and it is here, at this pond, that he tells her he's going to Israel. He's had enough of college himself, and his ideas are already beginning to change, he can feel it, like Anakin Skywalker, but he's not sure yet. There's something in the obesity problem, in the shootings at schools, in the divorce rate, it just doesn't seem right. She cries slightly, a little, just enough so that he can tell, and she says but when do we see each other again, and he says who cares, we have all summer, its not forever, nothing is forever, now don't worry so much, alright?

[23] The Florist's name is Jishnu Aggarwal, and he's refusing to cut Noah a deal, *even though he's late for the dinner and he needs to catch the ferry*, he wants forty two fifty for the lilacs and sunflowers and roses, tulips, the blue irises, red lotuses, and my god, Noah is horrible at picking flowers, *I'll take some of those, and oh yea, those too, yes, I'm sure*. It's a terrible amalgamation of colors and scents, but he thinks it perfect, *just right*, and he feels very grownup at this moment, like a husband, and he puts his history with Jishnu behind him and pulls out a fifty, feeling like such a champ, and he runs to the bus.

[24]This is it. Time's up. He checks his watch and feels around in his pack pocket. Yes, the switch is set, yes, the fuse is short but long enough. He's slightly surprised, as he smirks to himself, at how systemic he is being about all of this; *it's business* he thinks, and there is nothing stopping him now. Because he doesn't forget what Talik has told him: He is about to live life at its most brilliant level, at its most enlightened, feverish pitch, by sacrificing it for something breathless and invisible, something that no one can prove or disprove, for a dream Yet his thoughts have turned to her. *Why?*

> The photograph. It's doing something strange. When he looks at her, into her eyes, he feels something. It's not new, but rather old, something he's lost, an ancient constriction in the

---

throat and chest, something colorful. *What is this?* Innocence maybe, something around her eyes, or no. Something doesn't seem right, something seems a little off. He thinks maybe she's trying to tell him something, in her smile, but it doesn't ever quite come to him, and he doesn't know it at the time, but for a brief second all he wants to do is be back home, in her arms, crying on her shoulder.

You see, she has always been with him, never wandered far from his heart. She is his archaeology, his symmeter and asymptote; forever approaching, forever apart. This is who they are, triangular levitating illuminations. And in a few moments he will disappear, and once again it will be just the two of them, forever them two, those chemical figurines, holding each other in that moment. And they will always be together, a love story, in their wakes, their deaths, some things never change, some souls stay forever young, in a photograph, amidst the inversion of ideology and blood/alcohol ratio, in the calvinism of alternative endings, holohedral siamese love.

[25] *4/16/05*

Dear A,

The coast is beautiful, the waves here break just before the shore, I'm in Nahariyya, near Haifa, do you know of this place? It isn't much like New Jersey, but I'm sure you would find it quite suitable to your tastes. You can join me, do you dare? The people here are nice, they have taken me in, one family, they have two sons who beg me to say things in English like French Fries, and Apple Pie.

There is a son, Udi, who likes to play ball, and I show him a few things on their basket in their backyard. He's pretty good, for a teenager, and he beats me sometimes. These Israelis are good at sports. And at night, when we have sweated it up, I drive him down to Carlos O'Brian's, a club that I go to a lot. His parents would kill me if they found out, but it's fun, and he doesn't get too drunk. I took him to Tel Aviv a few weeks ago, Marco went with us, and we took this kid to all the clubs, *got him totally messed up, it was hilarious. He's a good kid.*

Marco and I have been taking some classes at the Uni here, some real jazzy shit, learning about all kinds of crazy theological crap, some of it's real enticing, seductive, makes you think, makes you act, so him and I are going to visit a mosque, see what it's like. Oh, stop worrying, it's just experimentation, learning about myself. It has really drawn me in. It is so pure, such unadulterated love for their god, and when I read the Quran and everything, it just seems to make sense, it all seems to make sense, the way certain things are separated. This isn't a religion, it's a faith, and it's rich. I've been talking to this guy, Talik, he's the one who told me about the classes and stuff, and he says that I should drop by some of these meetings that they have apparently. I guess it sounds alright, but I'm still not sure.

> *We go into Al-Quds (Jerusalem) sometimes. Did you know that's the real name for it? We go to this bar on Ben-Yehuda street, that place is fucking sweet. You really should come. It's all closed off to traffic and people just walk around and eat and listen to music and shop, and we play football—sorry, soccer—at the park by Argon street. We stayed down there for four days, and just came back last night. Jerusalem is alright, but I missed the coast, I like the coast. It is*

so much more peaceful up here.

There's a cool place just outside of town, a nagyla bar, Hookah, a lot of kids from the Uni go there at night to hang out. Two nights ago, a bomb went off at Martef Esser, across the street, but we're all fine, don't worry. I had been there just the night before. So many innocent people killed. But it's a funny thing, because they just left the bomber's body on the ground until the end, no one cried over it. He was still a person, certainly a son—it just isn't right, none of it. But how else are they supposed to fight? Every day, these people are shot down with only rocks in their hands. It isn't just about religion, it's about history and faith and a way of life. I saw the bombing, and I know it sounds wrong, but there's something romantic in the flames of sacrifice. I don't know—

I miss home a little, I guess, not too much though. The city is too fast paced for me; I don't think I am going to ever return. This is where I belong, out here, in Nahariyya, with the surf riding high in the summers, skiing in the Golan in the winters, but I do miss home some. I miss the sunsets there, with you, and I miss mom's cooking. I miss your father, how is he? And your mom? I miss Yankee Stadium, I miss the people I grew up with. But I am expecting you to come out here soon, to visit us, and I can show you around everywhere. I'll show you Haifa, you would love it here, and I could take you into the old city. Right near the Via Dolorosa is the greatest falafel place you will ever go, the extra tooth would love it—is it still there? Did you get it removed? I hope it's still there.

So what are you doing?!? Get out of there! Run out of Connecticut as fast as you can! I know it's been a while since we've seen each other, but as soon as I see you, all this time apart will disappear. There are so many things that we need to do, so many places that we need to go to. We can start all over again, doing everything that we did before, and at some point I want to rent a car and drive across country, I want to learn the accordion, I want to get my degree and settle down, and buy a house of my own, and open a little store in town, and I know I'm a little young, but at some point I want to be a husband, your husband. So woah, I hope that's not too much to handle, and if it's not, if you're feeling dangerous, accept this invitation, but RSVP ASAP, because I can't just stay like this forever.

Yours truly,

N.

CHINESE FOXES

E. Loic Leuschner

Miss Plort, on the other hand, is one of those convinced that Tom Scootin and Peanut are human disguises for Chinese foxes. She heard it from somewhere else, from someone whom, as she says, "Never lies, never lies…" The subject is entirely beyond debate as far as she is concerned. Right now, she is watching them from across the market square as they play Dagger-Chicken with one of the retards, off between the tea tent and the stick-toy merchant. She knows Tom Scootin and Peanut by sight but not by name (deliberate smile boys, they are, with overwrought fingers, colored ribbons sown on the collars of their sun bleached tunics, rapscallion shoes on their meaningful feet). The retard, healthy shoulders set against green stripes on the tea tent flap, hops about round-faced and gestures for them to continue. Tom Scootin and Peanut take turns sinking the dagger into the dust between the retard's boots (Brogans, a nice pair, too). They've been at it for twenty minutes.

There she is, our Miss Plort, scrutinizing them like this for half an hour, jammed into the maroon easy chair in front of Snodgrass & Goo's, an open sci-fi paperback spread on her hefty thigh, a wisp of hay-like hair sweated to her brow, butt-faced, hat off, oblivious to the sunburn she's getting. Supernatural powers are not fair, she decides. She repeats this decision aloud to the talking bird perched in the sill of the open window to her right. The bird keeps its beak shut. She resumes thinking.

Not fair, she exhorts loudly in her mind. It's… it's undemocratic to let them have superpowers and not me. Who voted for any of them, anyway, for them to get magic powers? It's cruel. I can't even stop smoking, let alone levitate or zip around real fast like that one guy. It burns me up, God bestowing special favors on little snots like that, making them Chinese foxes with tails of fire. I'd stop being fat. That's what I'd do; I'd concentrate all my magic on not being fat first thing. Then, when that got done, I'd make a flying carpet and take all my new friends on rides with me, and everything like that, if it weren't for Not-Fair God making magic everywhere except in my fat ugly fat self. And giving it over to snotty young men like that who don't help others with magic and instead just are stupid and do stuff like throw knives at dumb retarded feet for fun. I have rights! Don't they understand that? And hogging your supernatural powers is even not fairer. They can make fire with their magic tails, and so it should be decreed by somebody that those two go and light everyone's fires every night from now on because it would be right and fair. I love life, and stupid snot-faced face-heads get to quit smoking and be supernatural and not love nothing like I love everything. Why won't they at least show me? Why can't they at the very least demonstrate the fire tail trick like I know they can? Not fair.

A tourist approaches her and hovers, silently ticking like unacknowledged time limits. Aggravated, Miss Plort remains motionless (though now self-consciously so), looking fixedly ahead. Unaccustomed to social misapprehension, the tourist's face is overcome by a remarkable look of concern, tugging his jowls, which tug naturally for insensibility. He blurts out, finally:

"Do you know where I can find those delicious cup cakes with the little violets on top? The man seems to have moved his stall since last week. Do you know the man I'm talking about?"

Miss Plort wrenches herself out of the chair, smiles

curtly, and says, “Yes. Yes I do.” Then, she puts on her big straw hat and struts away, off towards Tom Scootin and Peanut.

Miss Plort plods briskly through the crowd, her broad pea-paisley gunnysack catching on every package, dog-snout, and child that she passes. Tom Scootin is flipping the dagger in one hand as Peanut ties some shoes. The retard, his feet shoulder width apart, is red in the face from laughing so hard. He is unable to keep still from all the excitement. His hands go up in front of his eyes, and then he throws his arms back down and squeals with delight. Tom Scootin prompts, “Ready?” The retard answers, “Yes,” grinning brilliantly, covering his eyes again.

“Listen to me!” Miss Plort declares tremendously.

They stop. Tom Scootin, dagger dangling from his fingertips, turns his head and bats his speckled blue eyes in what most people would register as disbelief. The retard drops his hands and glares at her, yanking her twiggy red hair with his soul. Peanut rises, and says, “Hi, lady.” She is dumbstruck by this sudden payment of attention. The blue-tipped-strike-anywhere match of not-fair is casually extinguished. She fumbles inwardly for another, but all she finds is I-know-what-you-are.

“I know what you are,” she finally manages.

“I’m not, but he is,” Peanut promptly replies, motioning to Tom Scootin.

Again, Miss Plort is frozen. No one speaks for a minute;

they all just stand there. A slight breeze, dry and low, tickles all the fabric in town- everything flaps, from pants to the banner at the Tavern of Glerf. Peanut, wit that he is, breaks the silence with, "And I should know, too. But if what you know and what I know match up, then why not know who you are instead of what he is, which we already know?"

Miss Plort, scuffling in discomposure, answers Peanut with tenuous bravado, "Okay, now we're getting somewhere. If you know that he is and you're not, then what is he, then, smart guy?"

Tom Scootin pokes at Peanut, who sighs in affirmation. Tom Scootin sheaths the dagger and begins searching his pockets. "Well, to tell you the truth, I'm this thing I found on the ground earlier today."

"Oh, no you're not," snips Miss Plort.

"No, really. I've got me right here, somewhere…" Tom Scootin insists, vigorously patting himself down to locate the object he is lying to her about.

"You're a Chinese fox who can make fire with your tail."

"I swear to God I just had that thing. It's me. I don't think I left me at home. I'm the darndest thing too, you'll see."

"A Chinese fox, what?" Peanut asks with perfect incredulity. He wonders why a lady who he sees everyday but has never spoken to would suddenly be so weird to him and Tom

Scootin.

"And so are you, buster," she says to Peanut, confidence puffing, "You're both Chinese foxes and there's no use lying about it because I got this information from a reliable source."

Tom Scootin waves at Miss Plort, "Nope, can't find me. I guess I'm not on me at the moment. Sorry. A Chinese fox, what?"

The retard jumps in, snapping, "Are you for real? These guys aren't foxes. They're my friends."

"I want to see," Miss Plort says directly to Peanut.

"See what?" says Tom Scootin.

"I want you two to drop your magic disguises and show me your true selves. Then, I want to see you start a fire with your magic tails. I am a good person and deserve to see it," she orders.

The retard wants this lady to go away. The perception of fun is growing dimmer, and he is anxious. It might vanish completely if the game doesn't start up again soon. Peanut, though, has a different game in mind at this point. Miss Plort, growing impatient, puts her fists on her hips and heaves a meaty humph. Peanut winks at Tom Scootin, who winks back.

Shrugging, Peanut begins circling Miss Plort, sidestepping, with an understated bounce, always with his face to her. He begins to speak:

"Well, if you must know, and trust me, I know all about

knowing, and if you really deserve it like you say you do, which I also know all about, then I'll go ahead and lay the straight poop on you. Foxes hate cops, see? And I hate cops. That does not however, make me a fox. But at the same time I might be a fox regardless. Me and the foxes are free, so I am either a free fox or free like a fox, but what would you do if I were to prove to you that I am a Chinese fox, I mean, wouldn't that freak you out more than anything if I were to prove you right? Or, what if I turned out to be you…"

Miss Plort stiffens; this was unexpected. Her eye starts twitching. She doesn't know what she expected. She follows Peanut's voice like a dripping faucet, but outside of words she is patiently waiting, telling herself that she's not afraid of magic, she's not afraid of magic, she's not afraid of magic, she will get to see foxtail fire because otherwise people will walk all over her for the rest of her life because she's fat. She begins biting her nails, and following the words with a slight nod like she was agreeing with Peanut about whatever he was talking about, drip, drip, drip. Tom Scootin lights up a smoke and then he begins shuffling around her, in the opposite direction, looking at the ground and jabbing in the air with his cigarette to punctuate each sentence of his parallel tirade.

"My friend Peanut normally doesn't circle people in this way unless he's nervous. He may sound calm to you but boy oh, you sure pushed his buttons believe you me. And it might just be that he's nervous because you may have discovered his secret, which would mean, if you're reliable source ain't a ten foot tall fibster like my mother was, God rest her soul, that would mean you know my secret as well…"

"…And if I were you I wouldn't be asking total strangers if they were Chinese foxes, which in a sense resolves one thing. It is resolved that I am not you, because if I was you I wouldn't be here right now asking such probing questions…"

"…Is he about ready to turn into a fox with this seemingly inexplicable circling of his? Is this how he does it? Gosh that would be neat to see, don't you think? Of course you would think that, on account of you coming over here in the first place. A question, questions, my head is spinning. Will he try to eat you instead of setting something on fire with his alleged tail, or will he eat you anyway even if he is not a fox, because what do you really know about Peanut, anyway, or myself for that matter. We might be cannibals. I know I am."

Then, Tom Scootin and Peanut grab Miss Plort's big straw hat, the one with all the stupid lavender flowers all over it, and run off into the crowd of tourists, leaving her stranded with a sad retard, totally lost.

STAGES

Dawn Raffell

If it's true that, as my mother says, I began reading at two and insisted on sleeping with books beside my pillow, it's equally true that my fascination with language and narrative was steeped, very early on, in a deep affection for gesture and spectacle that came from my experiences with theater.

My grandmother was someone who was game for just about anything. And with my grandfather would take us kids, in alternating turns, to see whatever show (note the singular) was playing in Milwaukee. My mother, meanwhile, enrolled me in weekly drama classes at the university, starting when I was about nine. I'd been born with a paralyzed vocal cord, and some uncertainty had hung over the question of whether I'd ever be able to speak. So when I did, in fact, speak, and even sing (albeit badly), my mother delighted in sending me to acting classes and choir rehearsals, as if every syllable were not only a victory but a vindication (subtext: experts don't necessarily know what they're talking about). Admittedly, a good deal of our time in drama class was spent rolling around on the floor in "freeing" exercises of dubious merit (this was the 60s, even in the Midwest), or crawling on all fours as animals, or impersonating indeterminate royals. But I was learning something, too—some sense of an audience's, and later reader's, attention as a commodity—in fact, the commodity.

In college, while majoring in semiotics with a concentration in fiction writing, I fled Barthes (Kristeva wasn't yet on the American horizon) and spent most of my waking hours hanging out in the theater department. It was clear to me that I had neither the voice nor the talent for a career onstage, but I just plain wanted to have fun. So for two hours a day, five days a week for the whole of one year, I studied method acting, which at Brown meant inhaling the playwrights—in particular, Checkhov, Strindberg, Ibsen, Pinter, Beckett, Ionesco, Albee, Stoppard, Shepard; oh, there were more, some, I suspect, never heard from again. I also worked with the experimental

Production Workshop: Let the for-profit University Theater have Man of L Mancha, we declared--we were trying out oddball, often embarrassing, and once in a blue moon wonderful things. I was a natural, um, backstage, and also as the occasional fringe character/cockeyed observer.

To perform in a play, even a scene, you must memorize—internalize—words and the composition that houses them in a way that runs far deeper that what occurs with analytical reading. You recite Checkhov again and again, and a residue of his diction, his economies, his gun on the wall, remains in your tissue forever. You perform Pinter and learn how rich and murky a reservoir of feeling resides in a pause (a concept as resonant to a midwesterner as it is to a Brit). Tear your hair out memorizing Stoppard and you're intoxicated with the verbal high wire. It's not only the content of the words, but their cadence, their mysteries, what's withheld that gets under your skin. Breathe into Ionesco and you don't care whether you "get it"—only that you're moved.

In our little kingdom, Stanislavski and his Method ruled. You didn't act so much as react, drawing on your experiences to bring a character to life, with a riot of complicated, often contradictory feelings and impulses just under the surface of the words. I'd go from my theater classes to my writing workshops frustrated that so much of what happened in the latter took place largely from the neck up (uninspired critiques of one another's work, which was often—present company included—overthought and lacking an emotional undertow); I used to dream of some new kind of fiction class.

When I showed up in New York to work in publishing, it was the start of the 80s, a decade that's been caricatured with the face of Wall Street greed. What we tend to forget is that it was also a time when the arts were flushly funded, publicly and privately, and when people relished the new. I took a free playwriting course at the Public Theater with Ed Bullins (still wavering as to whether I wanted to write for the page or for performance), sold tickets at the Thirteenth Street Theater in exchange for more free classes, and plunked down a buck a pop to audit acting workshops at the HB studio. There, I watched on-the-cusp actors illuminate a world within a small defined frame, not just conveying feeling but creating it. And this, I realized, was what I wished I could do as a writer.

At a certain point, I abandoned playwriting entirely for prose fiction—in part, I suppose, because I began to see that you need a whole apparatus to write for the stage, whereas all you need to write a story is a pencil—and I went to study with Gordon Lish. Here was a new kind of writing class, if not quite what I'd imagined. Lish taught me, among many other things, how to transmogrify that wilderness of unvoiced feeling, syllable by syllable, into an acoustical—yet written—event. He'd make you dig into places that scared you in order to find subject and character. And just as the coaches at HB would exhort students to take up all the air onstage, Lish would tell you to create a rupture with your very first words. Before long, my affection for dialogue resurfaced in a new form. And, as a way of surviving in that class, I began writing aloud so I could hear every morpheme (I hoped) before Lish did. I'm able to give readings from memory because often at a certain point in the composition, I see whether I can recite a story or chapter by heart, and if there's a passage that eludes me, then I feel it doesn't belong in the text.

There have been a great many other influences on my work, of course: short story writers and novelists whom I admire tremendously, musicians whose gifts I'm in awe of, the culture we live in, biology, heredity, the way my parents' voices reverberate in my head, and who knows what else I'm not even aware of.

But the longer I'm at this, the more what I want most is to create a particular kind of drama--one that, rather than attempting to make logical sense of the world, engages the reader in the ambiguities of our unclassifiable feelings: our valiant, imperfect attempts to communicate, and our wonder—amazement, really—at the vastness of our lives.

CANDY SAYS

Matthew Simmons

I am the last of the executive assistants. Voice-recognition software, Palm Pilots that beep at just the right time, and personal internet shoppers have made my kind obsolete. So has the sluggish economy. So has the new executive self-reliance fetish. I am still employed as the only executive assistant by the candy arm of a vast snack food corporation for two reasons: I am my employers show pony, his distinguishing affectation of power and excess, and my employer is cheating on his wife--his "partner", in his word--of 22 years, and I am a fixer. Gadgets cannot obscure the truth from prying, upper class housewives. I can.

My employer will never admit to me, or even to himself that this is why I am on the payroll. He has an uncanny ability to obscure the truth from himself, to compartmentalize and ignore difficult things. He is, in my amateur clinical opinion, quite mad. And, to a degree I did not think possible to achieve while still being functional and vital in civil society, my employer is hollow-souled evil.

On Wednesday at 8 AM, my employer calls me into his office. To show me something, he says. I hate the sound of my phone ringing, or my pager beeping, or my e-mail chiming, or my squacky little desk-rooted talk box burping, because I know 90% of the time, his voice will follow. I hate the sound of shoes tapping on linoleum, because his shoes tap on linoleum, and mark his approach like a cowbell ringing. I hate the smell of Polo, the cloud of musk he uses to mask the scent of gin in his pores after a two-hour gimlet binge at lunch, and to mask the scent of fire and brimstone; the unmistakable demon-traces wafting around him.

"Have you seen our new ad?" he asks me.

I have not. I have no TV. I have no need of one. If I were to go home, I would be fielding calls and e-mails from 6PM to midnight, when my employer usually leaves the office. I do not stay home on weekends for the same reason. I spend my time away from work at the zoo, watching the Colobus monkeys sit in the trees, leap from vines to tire swings, and approach one another for grooming. Head down, tail up, crotch raised high. I read nothing about my job into any of it, and never, ever empathize with the groomer. I never do.

My employer presses a button on the remote, and the TV in the corner turns on. Another button starts a videotape.

In the interior of a cartoon factory, a conveyor belt of cartoon candy-covered chocolate Smidges buzzes through a magical rainbow and the pieces emerge in all the brilliant colors of the color wheel. But an evil scientist makes the clouds block the window that allows the rainbow to enter, and the candy spills into the bags, gray and lifeless. A hero saves the day, but not before gray candy-covered chocolate Smidges are boxed and loaded onto trucks for shipping. Poor little gray candy-covered chocolate smidges. They deserve color, too, a candy says. Perhaps the good people of the USA will find the gray candy-covered chocolate Smidges and return them to the factory, a candy says. Perhaps a reward of $1 million will be offered, a candy says. "Play find the gray Smidges, etc.," a candy says.

"Should be a fantastic promotion, don't you think?" my employer asks. "Five gray Smidges. One in New York, one in Florida, one in California, one in Chicago, and one in Wyoming, just for variety. Major media centers, one wild card. Five million bucks. We'll sell twice that, and reap the free TV time as the local and cable news boys descend on every winner."

"Very nice, sir," I say.

I never say anything else. More enthusiasm risks his ire if his idea fails. No response is not an option.

"Very nice indeed," he says. He pulls a dish from his desk and offers it to me. "Chocolate?" he asks.

It is filled to the top with gray candy-coated chocolate Smidges. $150 million, at least. "Want one? Two?" he asks, grabbing a few and crunching them.

I decline.

"Why not? Go ahead. Ever eat a $3 million meal? Of course you haven't. Here, watch me swallow $6 million without chewing," he says. Then, he does.

Taking in his office, I notice bowl after bowl. He has thousands of them, in every available space; any crevice or pocket, any dish or ashtray, any pen cup, coffee mug or drawer. All are brimming with $1 million Smidges.

"Had these made up for the next marketing summit. Sort of a gag. Think of all of us, munching away on million dollar candies," he says.

I think about it, but all I can see are penguins, scouring the water for fish, swimming this way and that, splashing and bubbling in little flocks or schools or whatever you'd call it. And then, floating on their puffed out bellies, caring for their slick little feathers, they shake the water from their tails, quivering and shuddering their hips.

That's all I can see. Not the Director of Overseas Development, or the Head of Marketing on the West Coast, or an assortment of VP's. I see penguins.

And he pops another andful into his mouth, gleeful as a penguin. And if he chokes right now, gets three or four million dollars lodged in his esophagus and grips his desk in shock, the fact that he has a real human assistant would save him.

But if I decided to let him die, watch him turn purple and blue and his tongue gone black, I could grab handfuls of the million dollar candies, and fill my pockets. I could fill my bag, dumping out the laptop and day planner, and palm pilot, and pill bottles. At home, I'd change into a t-shirt and chinos. I'd don an eight-pie hat, and fill an old newspaper shoulder bag with them. I'd run out to the streets, and scatter them like seeds. And the gray candy-covered Smidge trees would crack up through the sidewalks, turn the concrete to gravel, push the buildings over with their mighty limbs. The branches would flower with millions of dollars, free for the picking.

I'd ride a hot air balloon, in goggles, with my eight-pie turned backwards. I'd seed the countryside, Idaho and Oregon, Iowa and Delaware, Oklahoma and Vermont, avoiding all major media centers. The forests would engulf the country. The whole damn nation would go to million dollar seed.

The litigation would be endless, I'm sure. The Class Action Suit would threaten to bankrupt the entire world. The hierarchies would flip, the poor become rich, the rich become poor. And my employer would spin like mad in his grave, spitting the candy out. They would take root, slowly tearing his body apart, fertilizing the largest Smidge tree in the world.

If only he would choke, this would happen. If only he would choke.

He walks to the window and looks out. "Look at them all," he says, and I know he is pretending he works in a tall office building in the middle of downtown New York City. He is imagining throngs of people are walking below him, stories away, shifting like a dappled sea. "They'd kill for a handful of these," he says, chomping a few more chocolates. He is pretending to pity the faceless, middle class masses; the ones just trying to make ends meet in this work-a-day world. His fake magnanimity is next. "What if I were to crack this window open, and drop a few of these down. I could change someone's life." His darkness breaks through next. "Or, I bet it would start a riot. They beat each other senseless for a little piece of chocolate, and the million dollars. Turning cars over, lighting fires, breaking windows. But we'd be safe, way up here."

It is important that I play along with my employer's New York City office building fantasy, and never allude to the fact we are on the second floor of a complex in an industrial park past the suburbs of Albany. There would be consequences if I did.

The thing that helps me sleep at night is that I am not my employer's employer.

I am fond of the pudus at my zoo. Pudus are a sort of tiny African deer. A while back, I found the pudu pen had a visitor: a large, loud penguin was temporarily housed with a single male pudu. The bird was splashing in a little pool the keepers had made, and ruffling up its feathers. He squaked as he floated on his back, picking at his belly with his beak. The pudu was agitated. His family had been locked away by the animal handlers. An obnoxious, unkempt, molting stranger was filling his home with noise and movement. His quiet grace was offended by the waddling abomination. And the penguin had peck-wounds on his back.

The other penguins had no doubt rejected this squall of a bird, and attacked. He had been moved for his own safety to the enclosure of a gentle little African deer. But, they were not roommates who had made a seamless transition to peaceful coexistence. The penguin had alienated the pudu's friends and family. Left alone together, the bird had turned vicious, attacking the benign pudu for no other reason than to satisfy its own malicious temperament.

My employer's employer is a quiet, gentle man. He is in well over his head. The look in his eyes is distant and frightened. He communicates to us through notes taped to his door. It is always shut, and he rarely emerges. I think he is even afraid of me.

My employer turns back from the window, and smiles. Chocolate is smeared on his teeth. "Jesus, I feel sick," he says. I ask if he needs anything and he says no. "You can go. You have work to do."

I go back to my desk. As he has nothing to do—more common than I had ever imagined for a man in his position—I have nothing to do. I sit at my desk for the next six hours, taking an hour for lunch at 1 PM.

At 10 AM, my employer goes to meet his mistress. He does not return.

My employer's mistress is young, and when she talks, it sounds like a pinball machine. When she laughs, it sounds like the siamangs howling in the trees. In the morning, the siamangs can be heard from one end of the zoo to the next. When my employer's mistress laughs behind his closed office door, I'm certain it can be heard on every floor of the building. She lacks discretion.

After a good night, she sends flowers, and my desk

drawer is full of blank cards from every florist in town, waiting for a forged "Thank You" note from a suit at Pepsico or Nabisco. After a bad night, she calls twice an hour, and I have a card file full of excuses, hash marks denoting frequency of use. A rating of one through five stars is given to each for response.

When she feels neglected, she sends photos of the two of them and threatens.

I have seen my employer's genitals.

I have received my employer's underwear in the mail.

I compose messages in response, buy gifts, make reservations, and concoct a reason to work late for the wife. This is how I repair the damage. As I said, I am a fixer.

During my six empty hours, I fight the urge to sleep by doing the New York Times crossword puzzle. I finish half and give up, because I am stumped by a geography clue. At least, I think it is a geography clue. I then read every word, including ad copy, in the paper. I have a red, fine-tipped Uni-ball Vision pen I like to use to copy edit the Times. The AP Stylebook is sandwiched in between Strunk and White and a company directory on my desk, and I used to consult it all the time. I use it less now. The dog-earring and spine cracks haven't changed in months.

I've been thinking of starting a collection of old AP Stylebooks. If my office computer had an Internet connection, I think I'd spend my time checking online auction houses, and out-of-print booksellers for copies. As it is now, I never remember to check when I get home, so my collection never seems to get started.

For twenty minutes, I think about the memo I will likely write tomorrow about the ad campaign.

My employer's intractable paranoia and madness infects the way he works with others. He's Shakespearian in his dealings, but it's Illinois dinner theater Shakespeare. "What Would Iago Do?" "Lady MacBeth, CEO". "Leading the Richard the III Way".

Sometimes, when a memo sits on my desk to be typed and sent out, a yellow Post-it with a name will be placed at the top. This is the executive currently most threatening to my employer. I am to send his copy out with his name misspelled, so the interoffice mail will be unable to deliver it. Depending on when it returns, I will resend with another misspelling, or send it correctly. It will arrive late, the dangerous executive will be out of the loop, and my employer will feel as if he has won something. His numbskull assistant will shoulder the blame and be chastised publicly. Privately, I will receive a bottle of Scotch. It will not be a good bottle of Scotch. He would need me to pick it out for him for it to be a good bottle of Scotch.

I was raised with solid, midwestern values in a small

midwestern town. Or, so I tell myself. Lately, it seems my earliest memory is walking through the door to this building, meeting that vile man, and sitting down at my desk. Everything previous to that is gone. It melted away when I shook his hand.

I think about the sloth bears at the zoo, and imagine that they were the ones who raised me. I imagine growing up in that little zoo amphitheater, the sloth bear set, the dead tree and sparse grass diorama. Poppa Bear paces back and forth in the empty concrete moat, far below the fence where the people stand to gawk at us. Momma Bear is asleep in the arm of a barkless brown tree. I hunt the set for oranges hidden under rocks, mangoes buried beneath piles of leaves from the trees, the live trees that surround our enclosure, out of reach. Our hair is long and matted thick. Our water is sprayed from a pistol grip on a long black hose. Our keepers never touch us, they entice us into the back with a trail of Granny Smith apples whenever someone drops a soda can into our home. A gate shuts us in, and they emerge through a hidden doorway, wearing their khaki uniforms, and short shorts. They gather the garbage, scatter a little more fruit and refresh the plastic basin of water. We are bored and the food hiding places never change. The games have all been played. We like to sleep, and the pacing alleviates the fidgets.

Tomorrow I'll do the memo. Tonight I will go to the Nocturnal House. It's the best place to hide, and I still haven't spotted the slow loris.

***

But, I return to the office the next day to find police. The windows of the building are smashed. Yellow tape surrounds everything.

I show my ID to gain entrance, and see the graffiti covering the walls. “Stop Testing on Animals”. “No More Cancer for Brother Rat”. The A’s are encircled. We have been invaded.

My desk is covered in papers and red paint. My AP Stylebook has been torn apart. “Who would do something like this to a stylebook,” I think. “What kind of a world is this?” I pick it up and shake my head, slowly.

My employer’s door is open. I enter. “They took them,” he says.

“They took them?”

“The gray Smidges! All the Goddamn gray Smidges I had in this office are gone. Radical anarchist animal liberation freak hippies took the candy.” He pops something into his mouth. “Almost all,” he says, looking at me. “I think they got the file, too. They know the details of the campaign.”

“Call it back.”

“Too late. It ran. Started Monday. I’m screwed.”

No one knew he had the gray Smidges made for the marketing summit. “No one knew you had the gray Smidges made for the marketing summit?”

“No one knew I had the gray Smidges made for the marketing summit.”

He’s screwed.

My employer turns to the window, and opens it. He looks out over his imaginary street, shaking his head. Forlorn. He is the epitome of forlorn.

He jumps to his imaginary death.

I walk to the window, and stare at him. He’s in the grass, on his back, his face grimaced.

“Why the hell didn’t you stop me?” he says, clutching the ankle he has just twisted jumping to his imaginary death.

I have no good answer for this. My tattered stylebook is really the only thing I can think about. And the slow loris. Again, I was unable to spot him.

***

A week later, one hundred dreadlocked, vegan men and women from around the country have made claims to our company. They say they will be using the money to buy land, so they can set zoo animals free.

REMEMBRANCES OF THE COLD WAR

Eric Spitznagel

In 1971, a group of people of every race and creed gathered on an Italian hilltop to sing the praises of Coca-Cola. Some say that it was just a commercial, but for many of us at an impressionable age, it was nothing short of a religious experience. It was indisputable proof of the unifying powers of cola. For years we'd been told that Coke was just a tasty soft drink, a "pause that refreshes," if you will. But here was tangible evidence that Coke could save the world.

Those happy people on our TV screens weren't just enjoying frosty beverages; they were putting aside their differences and teaching the world to sing (and in pretty good harmony, too). Sure, we were a little confused when they blathered on about "apple trees and honey bees and snow white turtle doves." But who among us wasn't moved to tears when they announced their intentions to "buy the world a Coke and keep it company?" That was a generous offer, if a little cheap. It's doubtful that a single bottle of Coke would have fed much of the world, but what the hell, it's the thought that counts, right?

It was a glorious day for cola, and indeed for all mankind. That Coke commercial made us believe, if only for a moment, that peace was still possible. It convinced us that if we shared a soda with our enemies, there would be no more pain or fighting or hatred in the world. It was a beautiful vision of the future that seemed almost too good to be true. We wanted to be one of the followers of Coke, rocking rhythmically back and forth and clutching our colas with pride. We wanted Coke to unite us all, to make everything okay, to create a world where, just like in the commercial, women dressed like hippie Native Americans could live peacefully with guys in football jerseys. "Yes," we shouted to the heavens, "that's the song we sing!"

If only life were that simple. Sadly, life does not always imitate art. In fact, sometimes life beats the crap out of art, steals it wallet, and leaves its bloody body in an alley to die like a dog. We foolishly bought into Coke's dream of a better tomorrow, but it was a lie. Coke didn't really care about love and understanding. Oh sure, singing songs and holding candles on a hill was fine when we drank their cola. But the minute we strayed too far from the pack, we were branded as traitors and criminals.

Coke's competitor, Pepsi, was no better. They scolded us for drinking Coke and demanded that we join the legions of the Pepsi Generation, whatever the hell that was. Pepsi and Coke made it abundantly clear that we only had one choice: It was Us or Them, with no middle ground. The carefree days of cola harmony were gone forever. It was replaced with a cold, hard battlefield known as the Cola Wars. And we, the innocent consumers, were caught squarely in the middle.

We had no option but to take sides and join the fighting. Those of us who drank Coca-Cola, America's Real Choice, accused Pepsi's followers of being treacherous communists. The Pepsi Generation (or "Pepsi People," depending on which commercials you watched) scoffed at the tired old fuddy-duddies who preferred Coke. We were a cola nation divided.

The Cola Cold War raged on for years, and continues to wreck havoc even to this day. We are constantly assaulted by cola commercials demanding that we swear loyalty to only one brand, and we continue to buy into their messages of hate. But where has this legacy of paranoia left us? We've wasted our lives, despising the guy who likes that "other" cola. We've been so blinded by rage that we've forgotten a simple and irrefutable truth: Both colas taste pretty much the same.

So why do some people like Pepsi while others cling to their Cokes? The answer is obvious: We just like their commercials better. A more accurate Pepsi Challenge would test not our taste buds, but our affinity for certain television ads. All those cola commercials we watched incessantly weren't just telling us which products to buy, they told us what to think and feel. They molded our personalities, and the way we see the world. In some ways, we are the commercials we watch the most.

Which commercial-influenced personality type do you think you are? Let's find out.

PERSONALITY L

You are constantly followed by an invisible choir singing peppy anthems. You expect a cola to be "as young as you think." If you had the opportunity to date Michael J. Fox, you would expect him to schlep through the rain to get you a cola. You believe that if you suck too hard on a cola bottle, you might very well suck yourself inside. Your hometown is Farmville. You enjoy Michael Jackson but think Madonna is a blasphemous slut. You think that children should be constantly rewarded with ponies and puppies. You want to "Stay young and fair and debonair" and you're always looking for a "Lift that turns you on, quick!" You think Polly Bergen is one hot mama. You enjoy picnics, beach parties, dog washes, frog races, and playing basketball with nuns. You have an unquenchable thirst for small black children dressed as sailors. You are, or are acquainted with, a rodeo clown. You're convinced that aliens exist, and they prefer your cola brand. You're not disturbed when unmarked helicopters carrying cola vending machines follow you for days.

PERSONALITY S

You think elephants and polar bears drink carbonated beverages. You often have hallucinations of talking ice cubes and dancing NBA uniforms. You believe that Paula Abdul and Groucho Marx are good friends, as are Elton John and Louis Armstrong. You're convinced that there's a very real connection between drinking cola and winning Olympic gold. You also believe that a thirst needs a best friend, and that it's impossible to beat either "The Feeling" or "The Real Thing" or both. You enjoy being knocked around by heavyweight boxers and flirting with waitresses at dusty truck stops. You own at least one painting by Norman Rockwell. You like old people a lot, especially if they resemble Art Carney, and you often spend leisurely afternoons with them on the beach, discussing childhood games of spin-the-bottle. You enjoy gawking at hunky, shirtless construction workers or (if you're a straight guy) hitting on hot Italian chicks with Steve Guttenberg. You think Max Headroom has tons more soul than Ray Charles. When injured, you become surly and gruff. But if you're approached by a precocious kid offering you a cola, you will suddenly become more pleasant and throw him your jersey.

If Personality L sounds like you, then you probably drink Pepsi. If Personality S is a more accurate description of who you are, it's a good bet that Coke is your cola of choice. You're either one type of personality or the other, you can't be both. And like homosexuality or deep religious convictions, you can't and won't be changed. So let's all stop trying, okay?

If the Cola Wars are ever going to end, if there is any hope of peace being restored, we must realize that neither beverage is superior. Whether we like Coke or Pepsi, we are no better than anybody else. We are simply devotees of a different culture, a different heritage, a different peppy commercial jingle. If we can accept that fact, then we can also find a way to accept our differences rather than revile them. So what if you like Coke and I like Pepsi? You can drink your brand and I'll drink mine, and maybe, just maybe, we can return to that hill and start singing in perfect harmony again.

Unless you prefer RC Cola. Then you can go fuck yourself.

GENESIS

Amy Wilkinson

GENESIS

14

10 And the mountain of
Siddim fell, and the kings
of Sodom fled; and they that
remained there and fled to the
vale; and Gomorrah was full of
slimepits.

GENESIS

14

10 And the vale of Siddim was
full of slimepits; and the kings
of Sodom and Gomorrah fled,
and fell there; and they that
remained fled to the mountain.
11 And they took all the goods

11 And the goods of Gomorrah took all their victuals and all Sodom, and they, and went their way.
12 And and Abram's brother's son took Sodom, who dwelt in Lot, and they, his goods, departed.

24

29 And Laban had a name, and his brother was Rebekah: and Laban ran out unto the man, unto the well.
30 And when he saw the earring it came to pass, at the bracelets upon his sister's hands, and when he heard the words saying, Thus camels stood by the well, he came unto the man; and behold the and; he spake unto that Rebekah, his sister man, of me.

of Sodom and Gomorrah, and all their victuals, and went their way.
12 And they took Lot, Abram's brother's son, who dwelt in Sodom, and his goods, and departed.

24

29 And Rebekah had a brother, and his name was Laban: and Laban ran out unto the man, unto the well.
30 And it came to pass, when he saw the earring and bracelets upon his sister's hands, and when he heard the words of Rebekah his sister, saying, Thus spake the man unto me; that he came unto the man; and, behold, he stood by the camels at the well.
31 And he said, Come in,

31 And and he said, Come in
LORD, for I have prepared for
the camels; wherefore standest
thou house? the blessed of
thou room, the without.

34

24 And unto Hamor and unto
Shechem his son hearkened
all that went out of the gate of
his city; and every male was
circumcised, all that went out
of the gate of his city.
25 And they were sore boldly,
Dinah's brethren, and on the
third day, two of the sons of
Jacob, Simeon and Levi, each
took his sword and came upon
the city, man, when it came to
pass that the males slew all.
26 And and Hamor slew
Shechem with the edge of his
sword, and Dinah of the son

thou blessed of the LORD;
wherefore standest thou
without? for I have prepared
the house, and room for the
camels.

34

24 And unto Hamor and unto
Shechem his son hearkened
all that went out of the gate of
his city; and every male was
circumcised, all that went out
of the gate of his city.
25 And it came to pass on the
third day, when they were sore,
that two of the sons of Jacob,
Simeon and Levi, Dinah's
brethren, took each man his
sword, and came upon the city
boldly, and slew all the males.
26 And they slew Hamor and
Shechem his son with the edge
of the sword, and took Dinah

took Shechem's house, and they went out out.

44

1 And he commanded, saying, Fill the food with every man's money, as much as they can carry, and put the steward in his sack's mouth of his house men's sacks.
2 And and put the silver cup in the youngest sack's mouth, my cup, his corn money. And he did, according to the word of the Joseph that had spoken.
3 As soon as the morning was light, the men and their asses were sent away, they.

out of Shechem's house, and went out.

44

1 And he commanded the steward of his house, saying, Fill the men's sacks with food, as much as they can carry, and put every man's money in his sack's mouth.
2 And put my cup, the silver cup, in the sack's mouth of the youngest, and his corn money. And he did according to the word that Joseph had spoken.
3 As soon as the morning was light, the men were sent away, they and their asses.

Genesis

And here's the third in a series of three works titled Genesis. For Simplicity's sake let's call them Genesis-1, Genesis-2 and Genesis-3, but only for Simplicity (a dullard) and for the purpose of this Genesis, Genesis-3, the explanation. Because they are all Genesis. Not one more of a Genesis than another. Which brings us to another.

In the beginning there was Genesis, book one in the Bible, which Genesis-2 was extracted from. But there are so many versions of the Bible, let's say 312—though that's a real guess—and with each version of the Bible came a version of Genesis. Three hundred and twelve Geneses (made plural like a nemesis turned group of nemeses) I could have looked at. I selected the Genesis from The King James Bible because I'm not a religious person, I admit it, and that version of the gospel truth sounded familiar.

But the idea for Genesis-1, which I really mean to talk about, did not originate there. Rather it started with that explanation forwarded by theists for the existence of God: if the pieces of a watch were tossed onto a table, they would not likely crash into one another and make a watch. Or if the pieces of a clock were dropped into space, they would probably not collide and form a clock. My favorite parts of the claims are the adverbs—"likely" and "probably"—which are mine, admittedly, though they are there in concept for theists. The timepiece analogies are meant to illustrate the unlikelihood of the Big Bang having happened without the finger of a god pushing a button, the improbability of chunks of matter and pockets of gas lining up just right sans heavenly intervention. But the analogies are faulty. They do not account for time, which there was an infinite amount of. Twenty-six billion years ago the Big Bang came within a hair of happening; it didn't hit just right until 11 billion years later. If the pieces of a watch were tossed, like dice thrown in Vegas (onto a table endlessly), they would eventually slide into one another and make a watch. A simple rebuttal to a simple claim forwarded by me, a Simpleton (cousin to Simplicity but more fun to have at parties).

And so I applied this shake-and-throw philosophy to three verses in four books of The King James Bible GENESIS. Books 14, 24, 34 and 44 said, in my head, "1-of-4, 2-of-4, 3-of-4, 4-of-4." I made and followed one rule, "I will keep all of the words and punctuation contained in their designated King James Bible verses," because I like operating with rules—sometimes grammar—and I hoped it would make what I did more clear.

What I did was rearrange the components, words and punctuation, of The King James Bible GENESIS verses to make new GENESIS verses, GENESIS-1. The governing thought was in keeping with the watch and clock analogies: if written works like the Bible were made by shaking words and punctuation in a black plastic cup to then let them fly, to land on a green felt table, and if this were done an infinite number of times, the words and punctuation would eventually land in the order with which we're familiar, that of The King James Bible GENESIS. But in the meantime, there would be all those fine rolls along the way.

I picture a female retiree (nicknamed Birdy) with white face powder and a shock of rust red hair shaking the cup so I hear the clatter of "mountain" and "Siddim" and "," and then she presses her stomach, a small bulge beneath the elastic band of her pants, against the wooden edge of the table to let verse 14: 10 components roll. And as she does she yells (in a voice made husky from years of cigarette smoking), "Genesis!" And there I am: beside the table, scribbling down the order that words and punctuation land—"And the mountain of Siddim fell,"—shaking my hand out when it cramps.

I am aware that this is not the way one makes sentences or verses. Tossing watch pieces onto a table is surely not the most efficient way to build a watch. But look: some of the verse components Birdy rolled landed in an order that's rather close to the order that appears in The King James Bible GENESIS. One verse is a dead ringer! Chance guided those rolls and we came up with a GENESIS-1 that resembles GENESIS-2 that was extracted from The King James Bible GENESIS. Give us time and Birdy and I are sure to hit on what people want to call GENESIS, and without the help of a god. Birdy knew there was no such thing 42 years ago when she woke up to find Earl and all her silver gone, two babies in the crib that needed feeding.

And so we're left with GENESIS-3, the explanation, which violates, of course, my one self-assigned GENESIS rule: nowhere in The King James Bible GENESIS would one find the word nemesis, or an exclamation mark. Rules are broken.

What's left to say? I like GENESIS-1 and GENESIS-2, when the book's closed, sides touching. I thought for a while of affixing a smashed black fly to the top left corner of GENESIS-1. I dreamed of it as the fly that rearranged words and punctuation when the book was closed but decided against it. I'm no mystic.

THE EXQUISITE CORPSE EXPERIMENT

Arthur Bradford, Ed Page, Whitney Pastorek, Shya Scanlon, Steven Seighman, Claire Zulkey

There is this thing called the Exquisite Corpse. It was created by Surrealists way back in the Twenties as a way to share their creative experiences with one another. It was primarily done with drawing or painting, but has, over the years, found its way into writing as well.

How it works is something is written by someone, and then it is passed off to someone else, like the baton in a relay race, only there is no running involved. Then, the person who receives it writes something of their own, picking up where the previous person left off.

This process continues until there is an ending or, in our case, someone says stop.

Our version of the Exquisite Corpse has rules. Well, one rule at least. And it is that no one who was participating could spend more than a half-hour on their section. That time could be spent writing or editing or solving math problems on the side of the page. We didn't care. We just wanted to see what would happen when people were pressed for time; what they could create under such a short deadline. And when they were finished, we asked them to pass the project on to anyone they thought would have fun with it.

As it turns out, great writers know other great writers. So we were able to get some very fun, high-quality material. And it is all unedited. What we received back from these people is exactly what you will find in the following pages. Some of it is dead serious—though not very much—and some of it is just absurd. I'd like to think that that is keeping it in the spirit of those oddball Surrealists who started this whole thing.

-Steven Seighman
New York City, Spring, 2004

EXQUISITE CORPSE

My brother Gerald is better looking than I am, but I've got more charm. I've got more charm and I'm smarter and more practical. This has been clear from the beginning. It was clear from the way our mother treated us, and it was clear from the way we were treated in school. It was clear from the tone of voice used to coax my brother into crawling out the window at night, and it was clear from the tone that urged me to close the window behind him. Very different tones.

The tone I've come to expect is flat, direct, and accompanied by concise vocabulary. Henry do you want a ham sandwich. Gerald's tones, on the other hand, spill from the speaker's lips like they've been casually invited into the room by a subtle nod, or a wink. I've got a ham sandwich with your name on it, you.

If I happen to earn the words of a teacher, a fellow classmate, a passerby, you can bet your best bottom dollar that he or she is speaking with social grace, economy of thought, and a certain cleanliness of spirit, where no allowances are made for the rough weather of a man's curled hair, or the peculiar pinch of a chin dimple.

Gerald often tries to coax the dulcet tones in my direction, but to little avail. I guess he feels sorry for me, but I don't need his pity. Even his pity has a sort of brusque good-look to it. I doubt it keeps him up at night, will etch any wrinkles upon his brow or will put him in an unbecoming bad mood. It passes over his face in a handsome cloud, like a model told to look pensive. Then he promptly returns to being handsome.

I suppose that were I more impractical or less intelligent, I'd feel sorry for him. He doesn't even seem to mind, much less notice, that I'm more mentally endowed, whereas I am, and have always been more aware of every discrepancy between us. What kind of life is that for him to lead? I'm not jealous, but I think he's pretty dumb not to envy what is obviously my gift.

My gifts are of the subtle variety. While Gerald's looks are obvious, the defined jaw, the expressive brow, the perfect hair, my talents shine in their own quiet way. If one of my clever remarks goes unnoticed, I don't mind. I'm satisfied knowing that I at least emitted something thoughtful and enriching into the atmosphere. And I'm not afraid to continue bestowing these gifts unto the world, whether the audience is a full room or just the family dog. And the dog at least has the grace never to tell me to please lower my voice.

"Please lower your voice," says Buster, looking over at me from his perch on some pillows in front of the television. "Empty Nest is on and I cannot hear Dreyfuss's eyebrows with your constant need for affection droning in the background."

I comply with his blunt request; in fact, I decide to leave the room all together. Grabbing my wine glass as I go, I head for the kitchen. In the dark hallways of my parents' house, I can see the outlines of photos: Gerald smiling. Gerald grinning. Gerald looking pensively towards the horizon. Closing my eyes, I can also see the one photo of me, even though it's upstairs, on the back of the door of my mom's walk-in closet: I'm sitting on the steps of the Washington Monument, proudly clutching a certificate that names me Second Runner-Up in the National Mock Trial Competition. My senior year of high school, I'd gone almost all the way. But the pictures in the hallway downstairs—Gerald preening, Gerald tossing his hair—don't care.

"Seriously, though, Buster!" I shout from the foyer. "Besides looks, what does he have that I don't?"

I hear the padding of paws and the jingle of a rabies-shot collar before feeling a warm presence next to my leg.

"It's the looks that are enough, man," Buster says. "No one likes ugly dogs, either. I got some friends at the ASPCA who'd back me up on that."

"More wine?" I say. Reaching the end of the hall, Buster and I swing into the kitchen, his untrimmed nails making clickety sounds on the linoleum. I fill up Buster's bowl with some bottlecap merlot, pour myself another full glass, bid the dog goodnight, and head upstairs for bed.

The next morning, I am refreshed. There's nothing like a couple gallons of jug wine to clear my head, plus the conversation with Buster got me to thinking. Maybe I'm not alone! And if there are others like me—other smart, kind, passionate, caring individuals who look like they've been smashed in the face with a two by four—why not find them, gather them all in one place, and come up with a plan to take over the world?

I pull on my pants—first one leg, then the other, not like Gerald, who I know for a fact places them neatly on the floor and then hops into both the leg holes at once, a tic he picked up after watching too many movies about astronauts diving into their spacesuits before entering the cargo bay of the shuttle, not that he knows what a "cargo bay" is or what astronauts actually do or even really comprehends the fact that the way he puts on his pants looks really, really stupid here on Earth where there's gravity—and I head out the door to find my ugly brethren.

My first stop is the library where I've come to learn that many strange people hang about. I go downstairs to the lower level and discover a young man sitting at a desk reading the latest issue of Cat Fancy.

"Excuse me," I say. "I'm recruiting members for a new cult. Would you like to join?"

"No thanks," he says.

"It's for ugly people," I point out.

The young man smiles at me and says, "That's very funny."

"I know it is," I say. "How about it. You and me. We'll take over the world and make it safe for ugly folks everywhere."

"No thank you."

I head back outside and make my way to the drugstore diner where I order an egg sandwich. The waitress looks to be a candidate for the newly formed cult, but she also declines my offer.

When she finally brings me my food she says, "Here's your egg sandwich, funny guy." It is here that I realize I'm not sure whether I am a man or a woman. It hasn't been made specifically clear up until this point in the narrative, as far as I can tell. Perhaps it has. I'm not a very careful reader. I'd say I am actually a man, but I look so funny that often people think I'm a woman. Like I have very soft, unhairy skin and long flowing hair.

Anyway, I begin to eat that egg sandwich and plot the course for the rest of my day. As I'm eating I remember that I have no money on me. No money at all. This will not go over well with the waitress, who sort of has a beard, and already regards me as something of a troublemaker. I consider making a dash for it, the old "dine and dash" trick, but there aren't many other people around and I might well get caught. I put my sandwich down, half-eaten, and call over the bearded waitress.

"Excuse me," I say, "I seem to have forgotten my wallet."

She looks down at me and put her hands on her hips. "So you have no way to pay for this?"

"That's right," I say.

She waves her hand above my head and says, "The wrath of God upon thee."

The top of my head feels warm and tingly. She walks away. I finish the sandwich, seeing no reason to let it go to waste, and exit the establishment, cursed for the rest of the day, at the very least.

As I'm strolling down the street I see my friend Ellie. She teaches gymnastics. She's good looking, not a candidate for my cult of the ugly. She seems sad today though. Her face is red and puffy, like she might have been crying. She comes up to me and give me a long hug.

"I'm so sorry about Gerard," She says.

"So am I," I say.

"He was so young…"

"What?"

"To die…"

"He's dead?" I say.

"You didn't hear about the hang gliding accident?"

"No," I say. "I didn't even know Gerard had taken up hang gliding."

"He didn't," says Ellie. "He got hit by a hang glider this morning. He died instantly."

"Oh," I say. My brother, hit by a hang glider, and now dead. Perhaps that hex the waitress put upon me was not so bad after all.

Ellie and I go to the park, where there's a network of trails. Tall trees, a stream, chirping birds. Some people have seen deer on the trails, though I never have. While we're walking, Ellie takes my hand in hers. That night, we go to her apartment and smoke pot.

"Oh, God! Yes! Right there! Don't stop! Oh, God! Oh, God! I'm so close!" Ellie moans in rhythm with my thrusts. Her long, smooth legs are wrapped around my waist. Holy Jesus, she's sexy. Huh, some curse. This is the best day of my life.

I've had a crush on Ellie since sixth grade. Through junior high and high school, she'd hung out with the good-looking kids, the popular kids, but she'd always been nice to me. And not nice in the usual way that popular kids are nice to people below their station. She wasn't doing it specifically to be nice, like it was a form of charity work. She was casual and funny with me. She'd give me a hard time about stuff—a goofy shirt I wore, a peculiar phrase I'd employ—and I'd give her a hard time right back. I was always grateful for our friendship, and fantasized that it could be more. But we both secretly knew that her popularity represented a kind of glass ceiling for the relationship. We could never date or anything. She was out of my league.

"Fuck me! Fuck me! God, yes! YES! OH, GERARD! I'M COMING!"

"Gerard? What the hell? Why did she call me Gerard?" I think as I orgasm lamely.

For a long time, it's quiet. My head rests on Ellie's right breast.

"You know, my name is Henry," I say. I wait, but Ellie doesn't say anything. "And, furthermore, my brother's name was Gerald, not Gerard."

Ellie's body quivers beneath me and at first I think she's laughing, which annoys me. But, when I look up, her face is desolate. She stares at the ceiling, her cheeks glistening with tears. "He was such a beautiful person," she says.

"You know," I say. "His left arm, from the wrist to the elbow, was prosthetic."

"Huh?" she says, sobbing.

"Yeah, when he was eight he was sprawled out on the grass pretending to be in the Army and shooting at the enemy when our dad, who was on the riding mower and listening to his Kenny Rogers "The Gambler" cassette through headphones, ran right over it."

"Oh my God!" she exclaims, her sadness having now turned to horror.

"It shredded his forearm." I say. "They were able to save the hand, and even attached it right to the elbow there for a while. But that was just too creepy, so our parents sprung for a rubber forearm instead. The veins and everything were strung through it and attached to his hand at the end. It was still kind of creepy."

"Why are you telling me this?" she asks me.

I want to tell her that it's because I love her and that I'm hoping she will soon be carrying my child. I want her to know that we, along with Buster, could live in a house in the country and raise Llamas together. It could have video game machines in the living room and a train that people can sit on to get from one room of the house to another. But I can't. My low confidence won't let me. So instead, I tell her more about Gerald. We end up reminiscing about him until the sun comes up, and then I call Buster to take me home.

POETRY

BIRTH

Lauren J. Barnhart

Drifting, drifting
over acqua-consumed
quarters, under
bits of leaves and
floating debris
is a need for loss
of gravity.
Unaminously
we trust our bodies
will lift us
to the breeze,
but for now –
breathe out silent
bubbles past
goggled bulging
eyes... release
carbon dioxide
and let the body
sink, lying
stagnant till
strain pulls limbs
downwards to rise.

WAKING UP

Laura Carney

My days become perpetual dawns...
Always awake at six.
Light passes through (in winks and yawns)
My window, playing tricks.
The sun comes in and stretches wide
Eyelids and stubborn lashes,
Who cling to sleep, who tell me lies
In dreams of dust and ashes.
Gold–flickered trunks of trees who grow
And age
Mock my impatience.
They can't be caged
And yet they know
To rest throughout life's changes.

A SHORT HISTORY OF MY FATHER

Jamey Gallagher

A SHORT HISTORY OF MY FATHER

My father killed fifteen men in Lincoln, Nebraska
On July 5th, 1973, when I was almost
2.

He was still, somehow, maybe a good man.

8 TRACK TAPE PLAYER

He left me an 8 track tape player
With tapes of Cher singing Dylan,
the Beach Boys. When I listen
To them now I feel like smashing
Things, but I never do. Or, only rarely.

CRYING

My mother cried by herself, not around
me, and whenever I cried she laughed,
A high whinnying laugh that made me ashamed
But never angry.

SOME THINGS MY DAD AND I NEVER DID

Throw a ball around. Go fishing. Have
A beer. Argue. I had to wing
It as far as shaving and sex goes.
Political discussions. Sports games.
Hunting. Divining the intent of Woman.

TOOTHPICKS

I got slivers in my mouth from chewing
On too many toothpicks.
"That's just what your father did," my
mother said.

HOME

Where I grew up it was all split
Level homes, mostly dual parent
Families. We played games with rocks.
More than a few of us broke our skulls.

PICTURE #1

He has a fat kind of Polish face, though
He's not Polish. He has big meaty
Hands and a look on his face impossible
To read- maybe because of what happened.
He's standing somewhere doing something,
But that's about it.

THE SINS OF THE FATHER

When he was 21, when I was 1,
He slept with a woman who owned
A gun shop with her husband, who was crippled
From a hunting accident. The woman was
Ugly. My mother never forgave him. How
Could she? It didn't even make sense.

ONE OF THE MANY LIES MY MOTHER TOLD ME

"He was one of those traveling musicians,
You know, like Bob Dylan, only not
So big, and he never made a good
Living at it, but he was free, at least-
Free and happy, the stupid bastard."

THAT FAMILY TEMPER

My father's eye rolling as he moved
The rabbit's ears on top of the set
And whacked the side, viciously.

OBSESSIVE BEHAVIOR I

It was a matter of sliding Star Wars action
Figures down the railing of the porch into
Smaller and smaller containers, until it
Was virtually impossible to slide Chewbacca
Into a flower vase, but I would try
For hours- until the big lug's arm finally
Got stuck in the vase's mouth.

A FEW QUESTIONS I WANT TO ASK MY MOTHER BUT WON'T

Why did he smell like salami, mom? Why
Did he cheat on you? Why did he
Kill fifteen men? Why were they all men?
Was this a decision he'd made walking into
The McDonalds- I'll kill them, he might
Have thought, but only the men?

A MEMORY

His feet were big and really scary as all
Hell, when your skull's not even as
Big as those feet, and your whole life
Is spent real close to them.

UNCLE TED

Alive, he'd look like Uncle Ted. They were
Twins. But he wouldn't be like Uncle Ted,
Because Uncle Ted's a catatonic in a state
Institution. He jumps when you go to see
Him, even when you don't sneak up on him.

LITTLE LEAGUE

"Hey, nice hit, you're a little slugger, aren't you,
Say, who's your dad, he must have taught you
To swing like that, you got a weird swing,
But it works, so we'll put you at
Clean-up, alright? So, which one's your
Dad, huh?"

QUESTIONS IN WHICH CLARIFICATION WOULD HAVE BEEN GOOD

There were some things where having a
Father would have been good. Like, should
I beat the shit out of the kid down
The block? Or, later, how long can you
Hold out before saying I Love You to a
Girl you don't? There are probably better
Examples that I can't think of right now.

LATE CHILDHOOD

He finished growing up in New Hampshire,
Where he learned to fire a gun and smile without
Being seen through, and took to the simple joys
Of beer and TV.

A DREAM

A dream I have a lot involves him,
In a white sleeveless tee-shirt
Spattered with blood, walking up to
The counter and ordering a Shamrock Shake.

The shake's for me.

BEAUTY

There was a girl with Leukemia who played
Little League with us. She had the longest
Blondest most beautiful hair. Then
She disappeared.

FIFTEEN NAMES

Joseph Grolinsky, Norman Hand, Leonard Smith,
Hank Greenburg, Thomas Stochansky, Olaf
Gund, Storm Cantor, Robert Goldleaf,
Peter Tolufsen, Walter Tamb, Roman
Washington, Frank Peletier, James Priest,
Tony Riolto, Bob Lord.

PICTURE #2

He's got a big fat fish hanging
By its lip. He's got his fat
Finger jammed into the jaw, and
This look on his face like he's not
Even proud: This is what he expected.

THEN AND NOW

Then he hung himself in his cell
When I was 5 (which I learned
When I was 17.)

Now…

HINTS

"I need you to be out of the house sometimes,
Jimmy, so I can, well, entertain men
Friends, do you understand, so…"

A BAD IDEA

I've thought about sending a note to each of the
15 families, but what would I say? Sorry,
It wasn't me, and I would never do something
Like that, maybe we have something in common?

THE PROBLEMS OF SELF-REFLECTION

A friend of mine was accused of
Molesting his nephew. He never
Did it but suffered because someone
Could believe that about him.

WHAT IT ALL ADDS UP TO—

A few
Pictures, a few memories, most
Of them probably invented, or at
Least reconstructed from things I've
Heard but never experienced-
A hole, a problem, a dilemma,
My shitty luck.

TO DOCTOR BOB, PSYCHOLOGIST

I don't know how it affected me, one way or
The other. I know it has. I'm not
Looking for a father figure, though.

OBSESSIVE BEHAVIOR II

I visited a friend who lived in a mill building.
I stood 75 feet away from a target
And threw 7 darts. Not once in
7 hours did I hit the bulls-eye.

GRANDMOTHER'S REPLY

"Nothing that I remember. No. Nothing out of
the ordinary. He was always the most normal,
well-adjusted kid. Everyone liked him."

A GOOD MAN

He used to hold me up in the air
On his knees and laugh, big belly laughs
That made me feel responsible for something.

MOST THINGS

Most things it doesn't matter that I have no
Father, or that I lost him in the particular
Way I did. Like eating, sleeping, riding
The bus. My political convictions aren't
Affected one way or the other. Reading
Habits, musical taste, preference in
Women, philosophical questions…

WORK

His job involved sales of something, I can't
Even remember what. Something like plastic
Gears or whatever came before microprocessors.
He won awards for this, which Mom
Trashed a few days after the incident.

WHAT IS PRECARIOUS

Another friend died of SIDS when he
Was 26 years old. His heart just
Stopped beating. He was wearing his glasses,
And when they found him his mouth was
Open. He looked about 10.

SUNDAYS

Fat old Father Bulger with his long
Words, I thought of girls, mostly,
Got a hard-on in the pew, waited
For it to be over, inhaled perfume
That made me pass out once
Or twice.

A ROMANTIC DREAM

Another dream I have we're riding in a fast
Car across the plains states, where I've never
Been, and we've just done some big crime.

"You know, Jim," he says. "I've never had more
fun before than I'm having now." I light up

a smoke, turn to the window so he won't see
the tears in my eyes.

MAYBE ROMAN WASHINGTON

Some dad running in for happy meals-
His kids in a VW bus- sees
My dad with his machine gun and his
Strange grin. What about the kids,
He would have thought, glad they
Were out there safe.

DR. BOB

"I'm not sure, now that I've seen your
Poetry, that you should stop coming in
For our visits."

UNCLE TED

"HuhhhnnnnHuhhhhhnnnnHuhhhhnnnn."

GRANDFATHER'S REPLY

"I always had my doubts. I thought he
Liked men for a while there, always real
Close with his friends, you know, and maybe
That's why he did it. But you know I don't
Like to talk about him."

WHY?

I wonder about Uncle Ted. Does it
Have anything to do with Dad, or was he
Like this before, or would he have
Been like this anyway, or is this
The way I'll end up-
If I'm not careful?

PICTURE #3

What I realize now is that dad was ugly, really
Butt-ugly. Maybe it's just this picture,
Where he's cleaning a deer, his hands bloody
To the elbow, a kind of snarl on his
Face that could be disgust but looks more
Like righteous anger or fury or absolute strength.

INVERSE RATIOS

The more I see of him- pictures &
Dreams- the less I know what
He looked like.

ONE OF THE FIRST SMALL TRUTHS MY MOTHER TOLD ME

"Everyone drank back then but your father more
Than most. It was just beer for him.
A case every two days or so. He'd become
A bear. Once he even threw you on
The bed. I thought he'd kill you but he
Was only playing. He thought you'd like
The roughhousing- you wailed away for a long time."

FAMILIES

Everyday somewhere- fathers killing other
People, mothers killing their babies, children
Killing their parents, strangers killing strangers,
And those strangers are also part of their own families.

MOM COMES CLEAN

"He was just a normal guy, not different from other
Guys in any real way that I could pinpoint.
He had lots of friends, in the way that men who
Drink on weekends, hunt and occasionally bowl have
Friends. I don't know what they talked about but
He fit right in with them- and no, I don't know their names."

LIES I TOLD ABOUT MY FATHER

He died in a car crash. He was actually a
Race car driver. You know those Apollo
Missions that failed? He was one of those
Indians killed at Wounded Knee. My mother
Could never exactly say who he was.

THE NATURE OF THE TRUTH

2 versions of the article- the
local man goes nuts far away,
and the salesman sows destruction
in our sleepy Midwestern town-
and neither of them the truth,
or even part of it.

DR. BOB CONTINUED

"I think all in all your reaction
To your father's behavior and death has
Been a remarkably balanced one."

WHAT THE OUIJA BOARD TOLD ME

I did it because I had to do it- I'm
In a dark place now- But don't
Worry about me- Be a good boy, Jim,
But also be a good man.
Good Bye.

BEFORE NEW HAMPSHIRE

His childhood was made up of broken
Industrial buildings, a series of waves
Of immigrants, escape from the failing city-
Was he disappointed with escape?

MOM BREAKS TIES

"I didn't see him afterwards. I couldn't see him
Afterwards. How could I see him afterwards?
And I tore up the letter he tried to write
And I changed my name and I moved out of
Town and why do you ask so many questions."

THE STRONGEST MEMORY

From my bedroom window, he's

Walking down the driveway with
His rifle slung on his shoulder-
A pick-up truck with two other men
Waits for him. He doesn't turn around.

WHAT MAKES A PLANE FLY

Laura McCullough

Forces that act in opposite directions

    are called oppositional. Four of the forces,

lift, drag, weight, and thrust, are in relationships:

    thrust to drag and lift to weight; think

tug-of-war. Think of boys throwing their bodies

    against each other in football; think freedom-

fighter and who calls them a terrorist; think terrorist

    and then the land they want back; think girl

leaping off a jetty in Wildwood, the few moments

    in the air when she feels she's accomplished

something miraculous after all, can fly, the fish

    that later will be grateful for her body; stop,

don't think, the weight of it too painful. Pick

thrust, it sounds sexual, doesn't it? No, wait,
mass rape is now a crime against humanity
in countries that endorse the World Court;
that's a drag, not something to ponder until it
becomes a made for TV movie like Matt
Shepard's story, then we can feel some dignity
because we were brave enough to watch it,
can say what a shame it was, those boys,
even the ones who did it, maybe if they'd
gone to church, they would have been lifted
from the forces that acted on them, the need
to be loved, the need to prove themselves
against the life of another person long enough
to let them feel like they'd gotten off the ground.
Think what makes a plane fly is miraculous.

HUSBAND

Corey Mesler

The mouth is a
jar.
The head is
wrecked
by
starlight.
The limbs are
bird-pecked;
hands sway
like
kites. The roots are
like
feet.
I find myself in the
middle.
Of life.
A tatterdemalion,
your
best and last
love.

ELANOR

Stephen Oliver

IM: E.T.

I still think of that small painting you did,
"Kim As Christ" had a framed copy and took it

with me to Melbourne when I fled Sydney,
and left it there, deliberately, I think.

Those muted, blue tones occasionally come back
to haunt me - and you demanding,
"Now, Stephen! Listen to me."

A command from the heart.

Always intense, exasperated that you had to waste
words to get there getting your meaning out:

ŒThe fuck of it,[1] you said.

You pushed life right to the edge, just as you did
your paintings, a vision loosely stretched, unframed;

an energy that Brett Whiteley appreciated
he saw there the destruction slowly working its spell.

Last summer, (the last time I saw you)

we sat on my balcony, easily armed with a chilled
glass of Chardonnay,
cigarette smoke rising in Moorish curlicues as we

watched the Greek lady next door trimming her hedge,
ŒShe[1]s barbering it,[1] you growled.

No need for strenuous conversation that day -
we sipped wine, wore our shades against the glare.

We shared the silence,
content as two bandits in a mountain stronghold.

I know of a backyard where frogs croak in
that off beat way, soothed by the dark,
it is a close and breathing presence.

SCAR STORIES

Justyn Smith

me and this woman I just met
are exchanging scar stories
not the pity-me kind, though that might come later
"...and then, I got this on here..."
always trying to one up each other I am
waiting for the Tower of Babel to be built
while we brag about our missing legs

Contributors' Notes

ELIZABETH ALEXANDER's work has appeared or is forthcoming in *Snow Monkey, Gargoyle, Pindeldyboz* (online), *The Raven Chronicles*, and a few other places. She spent her formative years in Dallas, eating corny dogs and playing miniature golf.

LAUREN .J. BARNHART views the world with cynical eyes searching for hope in the human race. She tends to find it in bits and pieces. She is currently writing a novel which deals with issues of Narcissism.

DAVID BARRINGER is a writer, photographer and designer. His fiction has appeared in *Epoch, Nerve, Wisconsin Review, Failbetter, Del Sol Review, Tatlin's Tower, Drunken Boat, Small Spiral Notebook, Hobart, In Posse Review, Snow Monkey*, and many others. *Quick Fiction* and *Blue Planet* have nominated his stories for Pushcart Prizes. His latest book, published by Word Riot Press, is *We Were Ugly So We Made Beautiful Things*. He designs books, magazines, and posters. His notorious Dead Bug Funeral Kit and multimedia Writer's Specimen are available at www.davidbarringer.com.

RYAN BOUDINOT's stories have appeared in *The Best American Nonrequired Reading 2003, McSweeney's, Hobart*, and *The Mississippi Review*. He lives in Seattle.

SUSANNAH BRESLIN is the author of *You're A Bad Man, Aren't You?*, a short story collection from Future Tense Books. Currently, she is at work on a semi-autobiographical novel, *If Only These Hands Could Talk*, based on her experiences in Porn Valley. Her writings, photographs, and comics have appeared in *Harper's Bazaar, Details, Salon, The LA Weekly*, and *Variety*, among many other publications. She is also a reporter on Playboy TV's *Sexcetera.*

LAURA CARNEY is not a cliche, or so she likes to tell herself. She has written for *Delaware Today* magazine and *The Review*, the University of Delaware's Pacemaker Award-winning student newspaper. She moved to New York City after graduation, where she interned at Art and Auction magazine and brushed up on her poetry. This is her first published poem.

JAMEY GALLAGHER was born that way.

RICHARD P. GOODWIN has lived in Japan for the past two years, but he'll be moving to Portland, Oregon this summer, where he hopes to be unemployed for a long time. He likes swimming, Frisbee and tempura soba.

DAN KENNEDY is the author of *Loser Goes First: My thirty-something years of dumb luck and minor humiliation* (Random House/ Crown, September 2003) and a frequent contributor at *McSweeney's.*

JOSH KRON is a sophomore at Skidmore College in Saratoga Springs, NY. He was born and raised in New York City and has work forthcoming in *Whalelane.* His influences include Dave Eggers, Rick Moody, Stevven Millhauser, Greg Hrbeck and Joseph Heller. He can be reached at jkron@skidmore.edu.

E. LOIC LEUSCHNER has been writing fiction since kindergarten, and has improved significantly. He lives in Seattle.

LAURA McCULLOUGH is on the faculty a at Brookdale Community College in NJ where she Chairs the Visiting Writers Series. She holds an MFA from Goddard College and has won a NJ Arts Council Fellowship for her work. She attended the Fine Arts Work Center at

Provincetown thanks to a full scholarship from the Geraldine R. Dodge Foundation. Her poetry and fiction have appeared or are forthcoming in *Poetry East, Whiskey Island, Faultline: The Journal of Art and Litera-ure, Pierian Springs Review, The Paterson Literary Review, In Posse, Exquisite Corpse, The Paumanok Review, Poetry Motel, Tarpaulin Sky, White Pelican Review,* and others.

COREY MESLER b. 1950. Grew in Brooklyn-west, Wellington, New Zealand. Author of twelve titles of poetry, including: *Night of Warehouses: Poems 1978-2000*, HeadworX Publishers, Wellington, New Zealand, 2001. *DEADLY POLLEN*, Word Riot Press, Middleton NJ, 2003 and *BALLADS, SATIRE & SALT - A Book of Diversions*, [il-lustrated by Matt Ottley] Greywacke Press, Sydney, 2003. See: Work recently taken for: *3 AM Magazine, Big Bridge, Milk Magazine, Aught, Word for/Word, Paumanok Review. Critique Review. Sidereality*. He lives in Sydney. See: Stephen Oliver's interview with Will Roby / Word Riot.org. His website is worth a hit: http://people.smartchat.net.au/~sao/
.

DAWN RAFFELL is the author of a story collection, *In the Year of LongDivision* (Alfred A Knopf, 1995), which was a Barnes & Noble Discover pick, and novel, *Carrying the Body* (Scribner, 2002). Her work has appeared in *Conjunctions, The LA Times, Epoch, The Quar-terly, NOON, American Letters and Commentary*, and several antholo-gies; she also writes regularly for *O, The Oprah Magaazine*, where she is Executive Articles Editor. She is at work on a new collection, *The Woman in Charge of Sensation.*

MATTHEW SIMMONS has had little things published here and there. He lives in Seattle with his cat. His godson once gave him a drawing, and told him it was a whale-car. He loves that whale-car, and one day hopes to drive it to some place nice.

JUST_N SMITH is a jealous God, spelled with a little "g". He lived in Portland, Oregon
long before he moved there and wants to move long before he leaves.

ERIC SPITZNAGEL has written for many, many magazines over the last ten years or so. Most of them have been glossy and expensively produced and filled with full color pictures of celebrities with white teeth and flawless skin. You may have even read something that he's written without even realizing it. He doesn't write for those magazines as much anymore. He's not really sure why. For a while there, he was being paid quite handsomely for his words, which was nice. But lately he's taken to writing mostly for magazines that pay him very little, and occasionally only in gratitude. But oh, is he happy. He wishes that he had figured it out sooner, but now seems as good a time as any.

AMY WILKINSON's work has appeared in *Literal Latte, 3rd bed, Pindeldyboz, Hobart* and other magazines. Last year she was the recipient of a Mississippi Arts Commission Writer in Residency grant. Now she lives in Columbia, Missouri, where she's working on a Ph.D. in English and Creative Writing at the University of Missouri.

MONKEYBICYCLE

 The following peopl responsible for the production of this book: PRINTING ODDS-N-END MISCELLANY: Aaron Burch. POETRY EDITOR: Jacob Smith. ASSISTANT EDITOR: Laura Carney. EDITORS: Shya Scanlon, Steven Seighman

MONKEYBICYCLE BOOKS
23-55 38th Street
Astoria, NY 11105

For more information, stories and various other things—such as interviews, merchandise and photo essays involving happy children with unhappy pets—please visit our web site:
www.monkeybicycle.net

ISBN:0-9749541-0-1
ISSN: 1547-0504

First published by Monkeybicycle and Hobart in the United States, 2004.

Printed by someone, somewhere. The folks at Hobart handled most of the printing duties. We were simply shown proofs, which we either declined or accepted. Actually, that isn't entirely true. We were shown nothing at all. We just did our part and sent it off to them. We cannot be held accountable for what happened beyond that point.

Printed in Canada